The Secret at Solaire

Nancy, George, and Bess entered the adobe house where they would be staying at the beauty spa. From a large window the girls had a spectacular view of the Catalina mountains.

"Not a bad place to spend a week," George said. "All I want to do is play tennis."

"I want some fruit," Bess declared, eyeing the fruit basket on a table. "Hey, what's this?" she said, taking a small wooden box from the basket. "Here, Nancy. You open it."

Nancy lifted the lid on the box and dropped it with a muffled scream.

"What is it?" George asked, running over.

"A—a spider," Nancy stammered. "It's a black widow."

Nancy glanced down at the poisonous spider edging over the lip of the box. At the bottom of the box was a note, written in an elegant script. *Bienvenue,* it read. Welcome to Spa Solaire.

Nancy Drew
Mystery Stories

Available from MINSTREL Books

111

NANCY DREW®

THE SECRET AT SOLAIRE

CAROLYN KEENE

A MINSTREL® BOOK

PUBLISHED BY POCKET BOOKS

New York   London   Toronto   Sydney   Tokyo   Singapore

This book is a work of fiction. Names, characters, places, and incidents are either products of the author's imagination or are used fictitiously. Any resemblance to actual events or locales or persons, living or dead, is entirely coincidental.

A MINSTREL PAPERBACK *ORIGINAL*

A Minstrel Book published by
POCKET BOOKS, a division of Simon & Schuster Inc.
1230 Avenue of the Americas, New York, NY 10020

Copyright © 1993 by Simon & Schuster Inc.
Produced by Mega-Books of New York, Inc.

ISBN: 0-671-79297-0

First Minstrel Books printing February 1993

10 9 8 7 6 5 4 3 2 1

NANCY DREW, NANCY DREW MYSTERY STORIES, A MINSTREL BOOK and colophon are registered trademarks of Simon & Schuster Inc.

Cover art by Aleta Jenks

Printed in the U.S.A.

Contents

THE SECRET AT SOLAIRE

1

Welcome to Solaire

"Wow! This place is incredibly gorgeous," Bess Marvin said to her friend Nancy Drew.

"It sure is," Nancy agreed. She gazed out the window of the van as it headed north through the rugged foothills of Tucson's Santa Catalina Mountains. Here and there, Nancy glimpsed a horse ranch or an adobe house nestled in the hills. But most of what she'd seen for the past hour was an amazing variety of cacti and trees under wide blue Arizona skies.

The driver of the van, a weathered-looking man named Hank Meader, rattled off a bewildering list of different types of cactus. "That's a prickly pear," he said, pointing to a cactus that grew in round, flat shapes. "The tall ones over there with the curving arms are saguaro, and then there's cholla and ocotillo and . . ."

1

Nancy wasn't sure she could keep them all straight, but from other trips she'd taken to the Southwest, she recognized the cottonwood trees and the groves of mesquite.

"I never expected the Sonoran Desert to be so green," Bess said.

"Green, shmeen," said the heavyset middle-aged woman sitting next to Nancy. "Who cares about the scenery? I'm here to lose weight. And to get a beauty makeover, of course. I've been saving all year for this trip."

Nancy smiled and held out her hand. "My name is Nancy Drew. And these are my friends." She gestured to the two girls in the seat ahead of her. Bess had wavy, straw-colored hair, and George had dark hair cut short.

Bess turned around and held out her hand. "I'm Bess Marvin, and this is my cousin, George Fayne." George turned and smiled at the older woman.

"Rhonda Wilkins," the woman said. "You all seem so young." She frowned slightly. "Why are you going to a spa?"

"I need to lose five pounds," Bess explained cheerfully. "Besides, I won a week's stay for two. Only I couldn't decide which friend to take, so Nancy and George are chipping in for the cost of the third person."

"You lucky thing," Rhonda said enviously. "How did you ever win a prize like that?"

2

"Bess sold the most Solaire health and beauty products in the Midwest," George explained.

"I've been selling all fall and winter," Bess said proudly. "Fortunately, Solaire makes great stuff, so everything sold really quickly."

"I wouldn't go a day without their moisturizers," Rhonda agreed. "They're simply the best."

"If you can afford them," put in the attractive, dark-haired woman sitting on the other side of Rhonda. She'd been on the same connecting flight into Tucson as Nancy, George, and Bess, and had introduced herself as Melina Michaels. With her slim figure, elegant jewelry, and effortlessly chic clothing, Melina Michaels looked like the sort of person who could afford just about anything. In fact, Nancy noted, most of the men and women in the private van looked wealthy, which wasn't surprising. Spa Solaire was one of the most exclusive spas in the country, offering a complete health and fitness program in a beautiful desert setting.

Ahead, Nancy could see two tall wooden posts with a wooden sign hanging between them. Spa Solaire, the sign said, for Total Health and Relaxation.

Bess gave a luxurious sigh. "I feel relaxed already."

"Not too long ago, this area was all ranch

3

land," Hank said as he drove beneath the sign. "Until last year, when Jacqueline and Laurent Rozier bought the place and turned it into a spa, this was a guest ranch. Spa Solaire has a hundred acres here—complete with hiking trails, riding stables, pools, gyms, tennis courts, mineral baths, and the finest health facilities in the country."

"Sounds as if he's memorized that speech," George whispered.

"Probably," Nancy agreed. Hank, whose graying hair made her think he was in his late fifties, looked every inch the genuine cowboy. Nancy wondered briefly why Hank was driving the spa's van. He looked as if he'd rather be riding horses.

It's really none of your business, she chided herself. But for eighteen-year-old Nancy, who was a well-known detective, curiosity about people was second nature.

Hank pointed out the small adobe cottages, called casitas, where the guests would stay, and the new complex of Spanish-style buildings that housed the office, dining hall, and the various gyms and treatment rooms. Walkways edged in tile connected the buildings. Through adobe arches, Nancy could see courtyards with fountains and stone benches and unglazed clay pots filled with bright, colorful flowers.

"It's beautiful," George said, "but isn't it

kind of strange for a French spa to look like something out of colonial Spain?"

"The Roziers believe in designing their spa according to the style of the area," Bess said, who'd read all of the Solaire brochures. "This is southwestern style."

The van pulled to a halt in a parking area alongside the building marked Office. Nancy and the other passengers got out and found that they weren't the only new arrivals. A woman in a white knit suit was emerging from a black stretch limousine, her diamond rings flashing in the sunlight. Two well-dressed middle-aged couples were unloading suitcases from their rental cars, and a slightly overweight girl who looked about Nancy's age stalked out of a chauffeur-driven Rolls-Royce without a backward glance at her chauffeur.

"Lifestyles of the rich and obnoxious," George whispered.

"Not necessarily," Bess began. Then her mouth dropped open as a slim, stunning woman with high cheekbones and silver-blond hair stepped forward to greet them. "It's her," Bess whispered. "Jacqueline Rozier. She was a top model in Paris for years before she and her husband started running spas. She's even more beautiful than her photographs."

"*Bienvenue*. Welcome to Spa Solaire," said Jacqueline, leading everyone to a shaded courtyard where a small group of staff members, each holding a clipboard, stood ready to greet them. "I am Jacqueline Rozier, and this"—she indicated a dark-haired, handsome man—"is my husband, Laurent. Just to let you know, Laurent has recently received word that our new line of skin products is ready for distribution, so we will have a celebration to launch the new line at the end of this week. We hope you all will join us."

Jacqueline looked around and smiled at everyone. "Isn't that exciting?" she said. Nancy noticed Melina Michaels's eyes narrow, as if she were disappointed by this information.

Jacqueline then went on to introduce the other staff members. "Some of you have already met Hank, who runs our stables and drives the van. Beside him is Marie Cormier, who prepares our unique herbal wraps, and next to her, Alain Giraud, one of our personal trainers. And this"—Jacqueline nodded to a young woman dressed in shorts and a Solaire T-shirt—"is Kim Foster, our nature expert. They will now take you to your casitas, where you may want to relax and change before your personal fitness evaluation. Here at Solaire, we tailor our program to the individual. Each of you will meet with an expert who will determine the diet and exercise program that is best for you."

Nancy waited while the staff members read

off lists of names from the clipboards. She, Bess, and George were soon following Kim Foster along one of the walkways.

Bess glanced at Kim's T-shirt and shorts and stopped to take off the coat she was wearing. "Is it always this hot in the beginning of April?" she asked. "It was about thirty degrees when we left River Heights this morning."

"In Tucson our spring usually starts in February," Kim explained. "It's been in the eighties for weeks now, and all the wildflowers are in bloom. You're here for one of the most beautiful times of the year."

"Which casita is ours?" George asked as they continued walking away from the main complex.

Kim waved ahead of her. "Yours is the farthest away, closest to the mountains. That means you may have to give yourself an extra five minutes to get to your activities in time." She turned to Nancy with a smile. "Now it's your turn to ask a question."

"All right," Nancy said. "Why is a nature expert leading us to our room?"

Kim laughed. "Well, if you're on staff at Solaire, you get scheduled for two different kinds of assignments. The first is in your specialty, which for me means leading hikes and giving nature talks. Then there are a few hours each week when we all do more general stuff around the spa—pitching in wherever we're needed. Your greeting committee was made up of the staff members who didn't have a scheduled workshop or class going on when the van arrived."

As they reached the farthest casita and Kim began fumbling with the keys from her key ring, Nancy peered through the window. She saw three neatly made beds, a wooden chest of drawers and desk, and a round painted table with three chairs.

"This is great!" Bess said, looking over Nancy's shoulder. "The room looks really cozy, and there's even a basket of fruit on the table."

"That's Solaire's way of saying welcome," Kim explained as she opened the door and handed each girl a key. She brushed back a strand of dark hair that had come loose from her ponytail and consulted her watch and clipboard. "Let's see. It's almost three o'clock now, and you've all got four-thirty appointments with Dr. Benay, who's our doctor and nutritionist. That'll be in the west wing of the main building."

"Why are we seeing a doctor?" George asked. "I'm perfectly healthy."

Kim nodded. "I'm sure you are, but everyone here checks in with the doctor first to get the right recommendations for diet and exercise. The Roziers are very careful about their clients." She looked at George carefully. "You seem like the tennis type."

"I am," George admitted. "I can't wait to get onto those courts."

"I'm the dieting type," Bess volunteered. "I'm here for a complete beauty makeover. And Nancy here is a detective. She just got through cracking one of the toughest cases in River Heights. The police couldn't even—"

"Bess!" Nancy exclaimed, feeling her cheeks flush. Sometimes Bess was a little too loyal.

"Really?" Kim said. "You're a detective?"

"Well, I—" Nancy began. She stopped as she saw Kim's expression change from friendly interest to something she couldn't define. Nancy followed Kim's gaze toward the mountains but saw nothing other than a few guests walking along the grounds.

Kim glanced at her watch. "I'd better go," she said quickly. "I'm supposed to give a talk on desert wildlife. See you around."

The girls said goodbye and entered the casita. A vase of fresh flowers stood on top of the dresser. The beds were covered with lace pillows and bright, handwoven Mexican blankets. In the corner was an adobe fireplace and a stack of firewood. A pair of candlesticks stood on a bookshelf. And from the window over the table the girls had a spectacular view of the Catalina Mountains.

"This is perfect," Bess said, flinging her purse onto one of the beds.

George hung her denim jacket in the closet.

9

"Not a bad place to spend a week. All I want to do is play tennis and swim and then play some more tennis."

"I want some fruit," Bess declared, eyeing the fruit basket. She shook her head ruefully. "I'm not even here an hour and already I'm starved."

She walked over to the fruit basket and selected a large orange. "Hey, what's this?" she said, taking a small wooden box from the basket. "Here, Nance." Bess tossed the box to Nancy and began to peel the orange. "You open it."

Nancy lifted the lid on the box and dropped it with a muffled scream.

"What is it?" George asked, running over.

"A—a spider," Nancy stammered, her heart racing.

"It's a lot smaller than you are," George pointed out with a shrug. "What's the big deal?"

"It's a black widow," Nancy told her.

"Are you sure?" George asked.

Nancy nodded as she glanced down at the poisonous spider. It was definitely a black widow, edging over the lip of the box.

At the bottom of the box was a note, written in a delicate, elegant script. *Bienvenue*, it read. Welcome to Spa Solaire.

2

Courting Danger

The black widow scrambled over the side of the box and moved toward George with unnerving speed. "It's just a spider," George said, sounding as if she were trying to calm herself.

"Get back!" Nancy cried. "The venom from that thing is worse than a rattlesnake's."

"Isn't it supposed to have a red hourglass marking on its stomach?" Bess asked in a shaky voice. She had moved quickly to the opposite side of the room.

"I don't think we want to turn it over to find out," Nancy said. "I'm sure it's a black widow, though. I've seen them before." She looked up as a knock sounded on the door.

"It's Hank Meader," a man's voice called out. "I've brought your luggage."

11

Nancy kept her eye on the spider as Bess opened the door.

"What on—?" Hank began as he saw the terrified expression on the girls' faces. "Oh," he said as his eyes went to the spider. The spider scuttled out across the floor, and Hank quickly stepped on it. "That shouldn't have happened," he told the girls. "All of the buildings here are sprayed for insects, but sometimes they get inside anyway."

Nancy was tempted to tell Hank that the black widow hadn't just wandered in. Someone had left the spider for them very deliberately. But she decided not to say anything.

Hank put the spider outside and tipped his hat to the girls. "Got to be going now."

George waited until Hank had left before saying, "I think we ought to complain at the office. These Solaire people ought to know what's in their fruit baskets." She stopped and frowned. "Actually, maybe they already do."

"That black widow couldn't have been left by the Roziers," Bess pointed out. "They *want* guests at the spa. They wouldn't be trying to scare them off."

"I think Bess is right," Nancy agreed. "And we should report it. I'd like to find out if any of the other new guests found little surprises in their fruit baskets."

George opened her suitcase and pulled out a

12

short white tennis skirt and a sleeveless top. "I say we unpack and change into some lighter clothing first. Then we can stop by the office on our way to see Dr. Benay."

"Okay." Nancy took a T-shirt from her bag and began to pull off the thick cotton sweater she'd worn. She stopped as she realized that the sweater's sleeve was caught on the clasp of her silver bracelet. Somehow, she thought as she untangled the bracelet, this vacation wasn't starting out very well. She hoped there wouldn't be any more nasty surprises in store for them at Spa Solaire.

"You said you found this in your fruit basket?" The woman behind the desk in the office examined the wooden box and the note Nancy had given her. "And there was a black widow spider in it? That's impossible!"

"It was *not* impossible," Nancy replied patiently. She nodded to Bess and George, who stood behind her. "I have two witnesses right here. And Hank Meader killed the black widow."

The woman peered at Nancy from behind horn-rimmed glasses. "I will show the box and the note to the Roziers," she said, shaking her head. "I am very sorry such a thing happened."

"Has anyone else reported an incident like ours?" Nancy asked.

13

"Certainly not," the woman said indignantly. "I assure you, there has never been one."

Nancy and her friends left the office and headed for the west wing, where they were to meet with the spa's doctor. The three of them climbed a flight of outdoor stairs that led to a balcony overlooking the courtyard.

"Here it is. Room five-two-one. Alicia Benay, M.D. and Ph.D. in nutrition," Bess read the sign on the door.

The girls entered a small room filled with thick white sofas and lots of lush green plants. A young man with reddish hair sat behind a desk. "Please have a seat," he said, nodding toward the sofas. "After you've had your consultation with the doctor, we will prepare a diet and exercise schedule for you."

"I want lots of beauty treatments," Rhonda Wilkins spoke up. The woman whom the girls had met in the van was waiting on one of the sofas. She nodded toward a wooden door. "Melina's in there now. She's so skinny, they'll probably tell her to eat more."

"Maybe she needs exercise," Bess said.

Rhonda shrugged. "Doesn't look to me as if she needs anything."

The door opened and Melina walked out, giving the others a sulky look. "Your turn," she told Rhonda.

Nancy frowned. What was Melina's problem? The sophisticated-looking young woman certainly didn't seem very happy to be at the spa.

Twenty minutes later, Nancy was called into Dr. Benay's office. The doctor was middle-aged, with short, blond hair and a friendly manner. She examined Nancy carefully and then made some notes in a file.

"You seem quite healthy and in good shape," the doctor said at last. "I don't think you need any special regimens. The usual Solaire diet and exercise classes should work well for you. Just be careful to drink plenty of water and don't overdo things in the heat. It does take a while for your body to adjust to the desert." She smiled. "And with that reddish hair and fair skin, make sure you use sun block."

"I will," Nancy promised.

"Then ask George to come in, please," the doctor requested.

George went into the doctor's office, and Nancy sat beside Bess, who'd seen Dr. Benay first.

"What did she tell you?" Bess asked Nancy eagerly.

"That I'm basically fine," Nancy answered with a shrug. "I need to watch the sun and heat, though. What about you?"

Bess's face fell. "She told me I need to lose six pounds."

"But you already knew that," Nancy said gently.

"I knew I had to lose *five,*" Bess said in a small voice. "And I guess I was hoping no one else would notice."

Nancy felt a rush of sympathy for her pretty friend. She and George were lucky; they never really had to worry about their weight. But Bess was always on a diet, and she loved food.

"Anyway," Bess went on, sounding cheerier, "Dr. Benay says she's going to put me on the special Solaire diet supplement. It's a high-energy drink that fills you up. You drink it in the morning and then you don't need to eat anything else for hours. And I'm going to get a total aerobic workout in the gym."

"Are you sure that supplement stuff is healthy?" Nancy asked.

"Dr. Benay says it is," Bess replied. "And that's good enough for me."

George came out of the doctor's office a short time later and gave a report very similar to Nancy's. Then, since it was nearly dinnertime, the three friends headed for the dining hall.

The hall was filled with long wooden tables. Nancy, Bess, and George wound up sitting across from an older couple wearing matching sweat suits. The two introduced themselves as Max and Eloise Harper.

Although the dining hall was decorated in a Spanish style, the menu was French. Nancy ordered fish and vegetables; George ordered steak and rice, and Bess, who was determined

16

to begin her dieting, ordered steamed vegetables.

The food arrived a few minutes later, and Nancy looked down at her plate in surprise.

Max Harper asked the question that was forming in Nancy's own mind. "What is this— an appetizer? I didn't order an appetizer!"

"Of course not, dear," his wife said soothingly. "It's your main course."

"Really?" George said, her voice amazed. "These itty-bitty portions? I mean, they're cute and all, but—"

"They're special diet portions," Bess explained.

"But I don't need to be on a diet!" George wailed.

Nancy bit back a smile. George Fayne was one of the fittest, most athletic people she knew. Nancy didn't blame her for wanting a normal-size meal. She looked down at her own plate and lifted a bite-size piece of fish with her fork. Come to think of it, she wouldn't mind a larger meal, either.

"Don't worry," Bess said brightly. "We'll all adjust."

"Of course we will," Mrs. Harper said.

Mr. Harper muttered something about driving into town for dinner and left the table. His wife gave the girls an apologetic glance and quickly followed him.

Shortly after tiny dessert cups of sherbet

were served, Alain Giraud appeared in the dining hall, carrying his clipboard.

The personal trainer sat down at Nancy's table and smiled at the three girls. Alain wore his brown hair slicked back. His skin was very tan and set off his brilliant blue eyes. He was extremely handsome, Nancy realized. "I just received Dr. Benay's recommendations," he began. "And I wanted to discuss your exercise programs with you."

"First, could you discuss getting us more food?" George wanted to know.

Alain grinned and glanced down at his clipboard. "I'm afraid not. You're George Fayne?"

George nodded.

"Dr. Benay says you're in excellent shape. We can tailor your exercise program any way you like." His eyes came to rest on Nancy. "She said mostly the same about you, though she thinks you could benefit from some aerobics and weight training."

"What about me?" Bess asked eagerly. She was gazing at Alain with a look Nancy knew all too well. Bess was in love again.

Alain winked at her. "You're in my special lose-six-pounds program. There'll be lots of aerobics and toning exercises, as well as workouts to build your strength and endurance.

"If the three of you will fill out these forms with your preference," the trainer went on, "we'll make up complete schedules for you.

18

The gym opens at six for morning workouts. Also, I strongly suggest that you all take advantage of the hike that Kim is leading at ten."

Alain stood up and started to leave, then turned back to the girls. "And Ms. Fayne, you might want to check out the tennis courts right now. Two of our tennis pros are giving a demonstration."

"Why does everyone here peg me for tennis?" George complained.

"Could be the tennis skirt you're wearing," Bess suggested with a grin. "What if I meet you two back at the casita? I want to check on the spa store and get some sun block."

A few minutes later, Nancy and George began the walk across the grounds. Twilight was falling. The sky had turned deep blue, and the Catalina Mountains were lit with the red glow of sunset. In the distance, the girls could hear horses whinnying in the stables. The desert seemed vast and peaceful.

George consulted her map of the spa grounds and pointed toward the left. "I think the tennis courts are behind the pool."

They found the courts easily enough. A small crowd, including Alain, had gathered to watch the demonstration game. Both of the pros were excellent players, Nancy saw.

"I wouldn't mind playing with either one of them," George said, her tone admiring. "Except I might get creamed."

Nancy turned from the game as she heard someone asking about tomorrow's hike. Behind her she saw Kim Foster, looking flustered. "We're going to Reddington Pass," the nature expert was saying to Melina Michaels, "to Tanque Verde Falls."

Then Kim's eyes met Nancy's. "I was looking for you," she said in a lower voice. "This must have fallen out of your pocket on the way to the casita. I found it on my way back." She handed Nancy a blank white envelope that she had never seen before.

"Oh, thanks," Nancy said carefully. But her heart was pounding with the familiar sense of excitement that came over her whenever a new mystery began. Did this note have anything to do with the black widow spider incident?

"See you around," Kim said abruptly, leaving the courts.

"Right," Nancy said. A few moments later, she stepped away from the crowd and opened the envelope. Inside, a note read: Must talk to you on the hike tomorrow. Urgent!

Nancy looked up as she realized that the crowd was beginning to leave the tennis courts. The exhibition match was over. She saw George on the court talking to one of the tennis pros. Then the pro handed George two rackets and pointed to the training machine that fired tennis balls.

20

"Hey, Nan," George called out. "Want to hit a few balls, just for practice?"

"Sure," Nancy agreed, tucking Kim's note into her T-shirt pocket. She stepped onto the court and took one of the rackets from George, then did a few practice swings to loosen up. "Okay," Nancy said finally, nodding at her friend. "I'm ready. Turn on the machine."

George leaned over and switched on the ball machine.

Nancy looked down at her racket, checking to make sure that she was gripping it properly. When she glanced up again, her eyes widened in shock. It wasn't a tennis ball that was flying toward her, but a sharp-edged rock!

Nancy quickly stepped to the side, only to realize that more rocks were being launched straight at her. They were hurling out of the machine like ammunition. She threw up her arms to cover her face.

"George!" she cried, wincing as a rock glanced off her rib cage. "Turn off the machine!"

But George was nowhere in sight.

21

3

Unwanted Company

Nancy raced off the tennis court, ran up behind the ball machine, and switched it off. She'd examine the training machine later. Right now she had to find her friend. "George!" she called. "Where are you?"

By now, the twilight had deepened. Although the tennis courts were brightly lit, the land around them was dark. Nancy rubbed at the bruise where the rock had hit her and called for George again.

This time she heard what might have been a faint reply.

"George?" Nancy ran to the side of the path. From there, she could see the dim outlines of rocks and cacti and trees.

"George, where are you?" Nancy called again.

This time she heard a definite "Here."

Nancy finally spotted George sitting on the ground beneath a mesquite tree, rubbing her head.

"What happened?" Nancy asked.

"I was going to ask you the same thing," George replied. She rubbed her head again. "I was turning on the machine for you when something hit me."

"You mean some*one* hit you," Nancy said.

"I didn't see anyone," George told her. "But I think the person hit me with a tennis racket. The next thing I remember is hearing your voice and looking up into the branches of this tree."

Nancy peered closely at the ground, then used her hands to trace in the dirt. "There are footprints here, all right, but they look like yours and mine," she said. "Still, someone had to have carried you here. You're quite a ways from the tennis courts."

George began to stand up.

"Don't," Nancy said, placing a gentle hand on her shoulder. "Let me get help."

"I'm fine," George assured her. She gave a shudder. "Besides, I don't think I want to stay out here alone. If someone *did* knock me out and carry me here, how do we know they're gone?"

"We don't," Nancy admitted.

Together she and George slowly made their way back to the main complex, where they went straight to the office. "We need to see the Roziers," Nancy said quickly to the receptionist, "and you'd better summon Dr. Benay. George has been hurt."

Within a matter of minutes, both Jacqueline Rozier and Dr. Benay appeared.

"What seems to be the problem?" Jacqueline asked briskly as Dr. Benay began to examine George. Jacqueline wore a green silk sheath that matched the color of the large emerald on her ring finger. Even in a crisis, she looked cool and elegant, as if nothing could ever truly disturb her.

Nancy explained what had happened on the tennis courts and again described the incident with the black widow. She didn't mention the note from Kim.

Jacqueline's brow furrowed for a moment. Then she picked up the phone and punched in a four-digit number. "Hank," she said, "would you please check the ball machine on the tennis courts? Apparently, someone has tampered with it." Then she made several more calls in French.

Nancy watched as Dr. Benay shone a light into George's eyes, then probed gently at the rising lump on her friend's head. "Is she going to be all right?" Nancy asked.

"As far as I can tell," the doctor replied. "Although she'll have a nasty bruise for a few

24

days. Have you felt any dizziness?" she asked George.

"No," George replied, "and no headaches, either."

"Well, since you lost consciousness briefly, I want you to take it very easy for the next few days," Dr. Benay said. "And come see me first thing in the morning."

Jacqueline finished her calls and set the phone down. "I am terribly sorry," she said, turning to Nancy and George. "We have never had anything like this happen. I just spoke to one of our tennis pros. She was as surprised as you were. She and Hank are checking out the machine right now. I assure you, there will be no more incidents of this sort."

"Aren't you going to call the police?" Nancy asked. "It seems to me as if someone is sabotaging the spa."

"We have excellent security here at Solaire," Jacqueline replied firmly. "I assure you, it is not necessary to bring in the police."

Nancy disagreed, but George was looking a little white-faced, and Nancy knew this was not the time to argue. Besides, she wanted to do a little investigating on her own. "I'd better get George back to our casita," she said. "Thanks, Dr. Benay, Jacqueline."

The two women nodded, and Nancy led George out of the office. Nancy could hear

25

Jacqueline and Dr. Benay speaking in rapid French behind them.

As Nancy and George crossed one of the courtyards, the door to the auditorium opened and guests began streaming out.

"Hi," Bess said, joining them. "Where were you two? You just missed the lecture on eating healthy."

"That's okay," George said. "I can guess what they told you: Make sure you never eat more than a teaspoon of anything."

"No, silly," Bess said, laughing. "It was actually very interesting. They talked about how different body types need different sorts of food to keep everything in balance. I'm supposed to eat fennel seeds, dry toast, and lots of apples and hot ginger tea."

"Oh, that sounds nourishing," George said. "What is it with this place, anyway?"

"I didn't mean that was the complete diet," Bess said quickly. "Someone who's thin the way you are is supposed to eat milk, hot soups, and fresh-baked bread." Then she looked at her cousin more closely. "What happened to you, George? You don't look so good."

"Let's go back to the casita and I'll explain," Nancy said.

"Just a moment, ladies," said a familiar voice behind them.

Nancy turned to see Alain Giraud approaching. "I was wondering if I might escort you back to your casita?" he said.

"It's really not necess—" Nancy began.

But Bess cut her off. "That would be lovely," she said. "And you can help me tell Nancy and George what they missed at the lecture."

Nancy barely listened to a word the trainer said as they all walked back to the casita together. She was wondering why Alain had been so eager to escort them. Did he have a crush on Bess? she wondered. Lots of guys fell for her pretty, outgoing friend. But Alain looked as if he were in his midtwenties, which was older than the guys Bess usually went out with.

Then Nancy noticed something that gave her chills. Other guests were also walking along the moonlit paths in groups of two, three, and four. Everyone was returning to their casitas. And along with every group was a staff member in a Spa Solaire T-shirt. We're all being escorted, Nancy realized. Someone here wants to make sure that all the guests are in their rooms.

The three friends said good night to Alain at the door of their casita and went inside. Quickly, Nancy and George told Bess what had happened.

"Are you sure you're all right?" Bess asked George in a worried tone.

"I think so," said George, who was lying on

27

her bed. "But there's definitely something weird going on at this place."

"George," Bess said, "Solaire is one of the finest spas in the country. It's been written up in all the health and beauty magazines."

"Then why do they escort all the guests back to their rooms at night?" Nancy asked. "I'm sorry, Bess, but I'm afraid I have to agree with George."

An eerie, high-pitched howling suddenly echoed through the night. As the girls fell silent, the sound drew closer.

"Maybe *that's* the reason we got escorted back," Bess said, her voice trembling. "There are wild animals out there. Probably wolves."

"There aren't any wolves in this part of the Sonoran Desert," Nancy assured her friend.

"Whatever it is, it's surrounding us," George said. Even she sounded unusually nervous.

"Those are just coyotes," Nancy explained. "Honest. I heard them on a camping trip I took once. Coyotes won't hurt you. They're actually afraid of people. And they're not to blame for any of the strange things that have been going on here."

"Well, you did tell Jacqueline everything that happened," Bess said, beginning to change into her nightgown.

"Well, not everything," Nancy replied, then told her friends about the note she'd received from Kim.

28

"I'm sure there's a simple explanation for that note," Bess said. "Anyway, Jacqueline and Laurent have been running spas for years. I'm sure they'll take care of things." Bess finished changing and peered intently at her reflection in the mirror. "Goodbye, six pounds," she said. "By next week you'll be gone, and I'll be slim."

Nancy turned to George. "Will you be all right if I leave for a few minutes?" Nancy asked. "There's something I want to check."

"I'm fine," George said.

Nancy changed into a dark sweater and dark pants. Then, promising to be back soon, she slipped out of the casita and into the night. She stood quietly for a few moments, waiting for her eyes to adjust to the darkness so that she wouldn't have to use her flashlight. A thin crescent moon, surrounded by hundreds of bright stars, lit the sky. The coyote chorus had died down, and the night seemed perfectly still, as if Nancy were the only human being alive.

That's silly, she told herself. There were other casitas in view, most of them with lights shining through their windows. But there was something about being out in the desert at night that could make anyone feel alone.

Slowly, she started to walk away from the guest houses and toward the center of the complex. She was hoping to find Kim Foster somewhere on the grounds. Something strange was going on at Spa Solaire, and Nancy had a feeling that Kim knew what it was. Where did the staff live? she wondered. Then again, maybe Kim didn't live at the spa.

Nancy stopped short when she heard a rustling behind her. She turned and peered into the darkness.

Nothing. She must have been imagining it.

Just as Nancy resumed walking, she heard the rustling again.

It must be an animal, she told herself. Besides coyotes, there were rabbits, deer, and javelina in this part of the desert. Almost any of them could be making that noise. But why did it sound as if something were following her?

Nancy heard the rustling once again. This time, she sprinted forward, determined to escape whatever it was.

But she wasn't fast enough. A hand grasped Nancy's arm roughly and spun her around to face a blinding light.

4

Terror off the Trail

"What are you doing outside?" an angry voice demanded.

Still blinded by the powerful light, Nancy shielded her eyes and stepped backward. In front of her was a man holding a huge German shepherd. The dog strained at its leash, growling, and the man yanked the animal back. Then the man lowered his flashlight, and Nancy saw that it was Alain Giraud. "Well?" the trainer demanded.

"I was taking a walk," Nancy retorted. "What are *you* doing—trying to scare me to death?"

"What is going on here?" demanded another voice in heavily accented English. Nancy was surprised to see that it was Laurent Rozier. So far, except for his greeting the guests when

31

they'd arrived, she hadn't seen Jacqueline's husband at all.

"It's a beautiful night, and I was taking a walk," Nancy explained. "Until Alain and his dog here nearly frightened me to death."

"She was snooping around," Alain said in a clipped tone.

"She is a guest," Laurent told him, "and you will remember that we treat all of our guests with courtesy. You may go, Alain. I will see Mademoiselle Drew back to her room."

"I am so sorry, Mademoiselle Drew," Laurent said, after Alain and his dog had disappeared. Gently, Laurent turned Nancy back toward the casita.

"Then you won't mind if I take a walk," Nancy said, more determined than ever to find out what was going on.

"I'm afraid I do mind," her host replied. "You see, we have many wealthy clients at Solaire. Many of them come to the spa and bring their valuables. We must keep very tight security, so that our guests have no fears."

"Have there been problems here lately?" Nancy asked.

"Certainly not," Laurent assured her. "But that is because we are so careful. Also, it is rattlesnake season here, and the snakes prefer to come out at night. We wouldn't want any of our guests to risk a run-in with a rattler."

"So we aren't free to leave our rooms at

night?" Nancy said. She was having a hard time believing that a resort's security system could be so restrictive.

"On the contrary," Laurent said. "Tomorrow night, Kim will be leading a stargazer's walk. We will provide several escorts, and you may walk the desert trails in complete safety."

Nancy decided to try one last time. "Actually, I wanted to ask Kim a question about tomorrow morning's hike," she said. "Is there some way I could reach her tonight?"

"I'm sorry," Laurent said as they reached the door of the casita. "But I'm afraid that is impossible. Kim is off tonight. Perhaps you can talk to her in the morning."

"I'll try," Nancy said, opening the casita door.

Laurent smiled at her, and Nancy felt a little shiver go down her back. In the moonlight, Laurent's eyes were pale and chilling—as if he were someone who never cared about anything except maintaining his own smooth, careful appearance. "*Bonne nuit,* Mademoiselle Drew," he said. "Sleep well."

If I sleep at all, Nancy thought, shutting the door behind her.

Inside, she found George already asleep. Bess sat at the table, reading the spa literature they'd been given.

"Back so soon?" Bess asked, looking up.

"I didn't get very far," Nancy said with a

sigh. "First Alain and his killer guard dog nearly attacked me. And then Laurent broke in and escorted me back here."

"Laurent?" Bess said, her eyes aglow. "Oh, he's such an amazing man. Did you know he's the one who developed most of Solaire's fantastic cosmetics? It all started when Jacqueline was getting terrible sunburns, because she's so fair and all. Anyway, Laurent told her he'd create something so that she'd never burn again. Isn't that romantic?"

To Nancy, Laurent seemed anything but romantic. "Bess," Nancy said, "I don't trust this place. They have the staff escort us to our rooms at night. Then, once we're in here, they patrol the grounds. We're not even free to take a walk!"

"Laurent must have given you a reason," Bess said, frowning.

"Security and snakes," Nancy said. And Laurent may be the biggest snake of all, she added silently.

At nine o'clock the next morning, Nancy sat outside Dr. Benay's office, waiting for George. She, George, and Bess had all eaten breakfast together, then Bess had gone straight to the gym to begin her workout. If Dr. Benay gave George the go-ahead, the three of them would join the hike with Kim.

A few minutes later, George emerged from the doctor's office, smiling. "I'm ridiculously healthy," she reported. "No ill effects from last night."

"But she's still going to take it easy for a few days," said the doctor, coming out of the office behind George. "The hike is a gentle one, so I've given the okay for that, but make sure she doesn't overdo things."

"I will," Nancy promised.

"Let's go back to the room and get our tennis rackets," George said to Nancy.

Dr. Benay cleared her throat and picked up a Solaire schedule. "The hike will provide enough of a workout for you today, I think. Right now, I suggest you attend either the stretching class or a lecture on healthy makeup."

George groaned.

"Come on, let's go stretch," Nancy said with a laugh. But as soon as they were a good distance from the doctor's office, Nancy headed toward the tennis courts.

"I thought we were going to the gym," George said.

"I still want to check out that ball machine," Nancy said. "I know the staff here has looked at it, but I want to see if I can find any clues myself."

The girls approached the tennis courts. One

35

of the pros was coaching Melina Michaels, who was scrambling all over the court and missing nearly every shot.

"I thought she'd be a better player," George said. "Melina's the type who looks as though she were born playing tennis."

"Apparently not," Nancy said. "Can you distract those two? I want to have a look at the ball machine."

"No problem," George said. But as she and Nancy walked toward the courts, the pro saw them and stopped the game. Melina, looking very grateful for the interruption, left the court.

"Hi, I'm Lisette," the pro said, walking up to meet Nancy and George. "Are you the one who was hurt last night?" she asked George.

"I'm all right now," George said with a shrug.

Lisette wiped her forehead with a wristband and walked over to the ball machine. "I don't know when it was tampered with," she said. "It was working perfectly yesterday afternoon."

"Do you mind if we look at it?" Nancy asked, glad that the tennis pro seemed willing to talk.

Lisette shrugged. "Look all you want, but I don't think you'll learn anything. This morning one of the maintenance people took it apart, oiled it, and put it back together."

Cleaning off all fingerprints and evidence,

Nancy thought to herself. "Lisette," she said, "who could have tampered with it in the first place?"

Lisette ran a hand through her short red curls. "Nearly anyone, I guess. It's not a very difficult machine to load. I—"

She was interrupted by an announcement being broadcast over the PA system. All guests going on the hike were asked to gather in the main courtyard, wearing hiking boots or shoes with good ankle support. Those who wanted to swim were told to wear a bathing suit under their clothes.

"We'd better go," George told the tennis pro, "but I'd like to play a match with you sometime."

Lisette smiled. "Sure, anytime."

Nancy and George soon joined the other guests who'd assembled for the hike. Bess arrived, looking slightly winded but cheerful. "I had an incredible workout," she announced. "I'm feeling stronger and thinner already."

"Great," Nancy told her, trying not to smile.

"Hey, look," George said. "There's Kim now."

Nancy had been hoping to speak to Kim right away about the urgent note the nature expert had given her yesterday. But Kim was walking toward them, talking earnestly to Melina Michaels. A few minutes later, Kim read off the names of the ten or so people who'd volunteered for the hike, and then they

37

all got into the Solaire van. Melina was one of them. Nancy wondered whether Kim had just talked her into the outing.

"We'll be driving east across the Tucson Valley to the foothills of the Rincon Mountains," Kim told them as she started up the van. "Reddington Pass is an old rancher's road—all dirt and pretty rough in spots, but the only road that crosses that mountain range. We'll only go part of the way up the pass. Then we'll hike down to Tanque Verde Falls and have lunch there. If you like ice-cold water, you can go for a swim, too."

Almost forty minutes later, Nancy saw the dark, massive mountains looming in front of them. Patches of winter snow still lingered near their peaks.

As Kim had promised, the van soon left the pavement and began climbing a narrow, dirt road that seemed to spiral straight up into the sky.

Bess looked at the sheer drop off the side of the road and gulped. "I'm glad I'm not driving," she said.

The road climbed and climbed, growing rougher the higher it went. Finally the road leveled off, and the van came to a halt.

As the group got out of the van, Kim handed everyone a paper bag. "You'll each find lunch, a water bottle, and Solaire sun block inside," she told them. "We'll be on a trail, but watch out for the cacti and snakes."

Bess gave a little shudder. "Maybe I should have stayed in the gym."

"No, you made the right choice," Nancy said. "Look at how beautiful it is up here." Wildflowers sprang up on both sides of the narrow footpath—orange mallow, purple lupine, and magenta penstemon were all in bloom. Tiny hummingbirds hovered near the flowers, while overhead a red-tailed hawk soared through the clear blue sky.

"These flowers are amazing," Bess said. "I never thought I'd see so many bright colors in the middle of the desert. And look, there's a jackrabbit!" Nancy smiled as the rabbit sprang by on long legs.

The trail snaked upward through the desert scrub. Somewhere below, Nancy could hear the sound of the falls. The morning sun grew steadily hotter, and they all stopped to put on sun block and hats. Then Melina got a cactus spine in her pants leg and complained very loudly until Kim got it out for her.

At last they reached the point where they could see down to the falls, and the sight took Nancy's breath away. The waterfalls themselves weren't very high. Actually, they were a series of low falls, swirling through a chasm of white quartz. The wet stone glistened in the morning sun, looking nearly opalescent. Two wide sand beaches lined either side of the rushing creek, and cottonwood trees grew in the center of the water's path.

"This way down," Kim told everyone. The trail had grown increasingly narrow, winding now between deep red boulders.

"We're lucky we have this place to ourselves," Kim went on. "Tanque Verde Creek doesn't run all year long. When there's water here, there are usually a lot of other people."

"It's kind of weird to see so much water in the middle of the desert," George said.

"Most of this is melted snow from the top of the mountain range," Kim explained. "And last week we had some heavy rains, so the water level is pretty high for this time of year. If you want to swim, be prepared for icy water."

"I think I'll take the Jacuzzi back at the spa," Max Harper declared. "Let's eat lunch." Nancy remembered Max as the man who had gone into town for dinner the night before.

The group sat down on the beach and began opening up their bags.

"Peanut butter, rice cakes, veggies and dip, and more high-energy drink," Max grumbled. "I should have eaten the sun block."

"It would probably be perfectly healthy," Bess said thoughtfully. "All the Solaire products are made from pure, natural ingredients."

Everyone settled down to their lunches.

40

Nancy talked for a while with the Harpers and an advertising executive from Connecticut named Richard Levine. But all the while, she was trying to find an opportunity to talk to Kim. Kim was busy giving the others as much information as she could about the wilderness area, though Nancy was sure that the young woman seemed a bit jittery. What was it that Kim wanted to tell her, and why was she being so secretive?

Finally, Kim stood up and took a small camera from her pack. "You'll have to bear with me. I'm an amateur photographer," she told the group. "Let me see if I can get some shots of all of you together." She took a few pictures of the group and asked Bess to take one of her and Nancy. Then Kim began to photograph the nearby rock formations.

Directly across the creek from where they sat, large white quartz rocks edged the chasm. "I want to get some shots over there," Kim explained. "I'll be back in two minutes."

This may be my only chance to talk to her alone, Nancy thought. She stood up and followed Kim, crossing the water as the nature expert had by making her way across some low rocks.

"Wait up!" Nancy called out when she was halfway across. She balanced herself against the trunk of one of the cottonwood trees that grew out of the water.

"Stay there for a minute," Kim called back. She had climbed partway up one of the huge rocks on the other side of the chasm. "You look great against that tree. Let me get your picture."

Nancy grinned and posed while Kim took several photographs. Nancy was about to walk the rest of the way across the creek when she suddenly heard something that sounded like a very loud roar.

That's crazy, Nancy thought. There isn't anything in the desert that roars. She turned to glance upstream, and every muscle in her body froze in horror.

A solid wall of water, taller than Nancy herself, was pouring through the narrow chasm walls, rushing straight toward her!

5

Rescue!

George's hoarse shout broke through Nancy's terror. "Climb," George screamed. "The tree! Climb it!"

Nancy's reflexes took over. She didn't stop to think about how to get up the tree. She just climbed as fast and hard as she could, pulling herself up into the cottonwood branches.

If she'd been one second slower, it would have been too late. The huge wall of water roared down the chasm. Beneath her, Nancy felt the trunk of the tree shaking as the powerful torrent swept past. She held on more tightly, gripping the tree with all her strength.

"Nancy!" She glanced down at the beach, where just a few minutes ago they'd all eaten lunch. The beach was gone, covered by swirling green water. Even some of the larger boulders were submerged. Nancy felt her heart

43

begin to hammer painfully. What had happened to her friends?

"Nance!" It was George's voice again, though farther away. Nancy sighed with relief as she saw the group from Solaire standing a good ways above the beach. Somehow, they'd all made it to higher ground. But their expressions were panicked as they watched the foaming water pour through the chasm. "Don't move!" George cried. "We'll get help!"

"Great!" Melina exclaimed angrily. "We're stuck miles from nowhere without our guide! She probably had the keys to the van. How are we supposed to get back?"

Kim! Nancy thought. Her eyes scanned the other side of the chasm. She couldn't even distinguish the exact spot on which Kim had stood, taking photographs. The broad sheet of white rock had vanished beneath the current. Nancy looked down and saw a small, uprooted tree swirl by—and she had an awful feeling that she knew what had happened to Kim.

"We'll be back as soon as we can," George called out. Then she and several others began to climb the trail that led back to the road. Nancy sighed and told herself to be patient. It would take a while to get help, she knew. They were nowhere near a phone—especially without the van.

"Nan!" Bess had remained on the beach, along with the Harpers, Richard Levine, and

44

Melina. "I think the water's going down!" she called.

Nancy peered down from the tree again. Bess was right. The water was getting lower.

An hour later, the water level was low enough for Nancy to climb down. Just to be safe, Bess and the others formed a human chain from the shoreline. When Nancy finally scrambled shakily out of the tree and into the knee-high icy water, she grasped Bess's hand and was pulled to safety.

"We've got to find Kim," Nancy said, rubbing her aching arms as she stepped onto solid land. "Kim!" she started calling. "Can you hear me? Kim!"

"I think these are the people for the job," said Richard Levine as a half-dozen men and women rushed down the trail. They all wore hiking boots, jeans, and neon-orange shirts and carried an assortment of ropes, walkie-talkies, and other equipment.

Nancy read the arm patch worn by the gray-haired woman in the lead. "Search and Rescue Association," Nancy said. "Thank goodness!"

Melina raced to the front of the group. "Have you come to rescue us?" she asked anxiously.

The gray-haired woman looked Melina up and down and scratched her head. "Doesn't look to me like you need much rescuing," she said. "You're fit enough to walk the trail out of here."

"Our guide may have been swept downstream by the flood," Nancy said quickly. She pointed to the spot she'd last seen Kim and explained what had happened.

"Well, that's the person we ought to be rescuing," a younger man said. Immediately, he radioed a message through his walkie-talkie, summoning more help.

"We want to help you search," Nancy said.

"I appreciate that," the gray-haired woman said. "But there could be another surge of flooding, and one lost person is enough for today. You'd be a bigger help to us if you all went back up to the road." She gave Melina a stern look. "I'll send one of my people with you, just so you don't run into trouble. The rest of us are going to stay here and look for your guide. We'll get in touch with Spa Solaire as soon as we find anything."

Nancy knew the woman was right. Their own inexperienced group would probably get in the way. But she felt awful going back without Kim—especially when Kim was someone who had needed her help.

"Nan!" Bess's voice was a whisper.

"What?" Nancy asked. The rest of the group from Solaire was already starting up the trail.

"What does that look like to you?" Bess asked, pointing to a large clump of mud and brush that had come to rest at the foot of one of the boulders near the stream.

"Goop?" Nancy asked.

"Don't you see it?" Bess hissed.

Suddenly, Nancy did see something. Sticking out from the very edge of the goop was the corner of Kim's camera. Nancy pulled it out. The camera was totally covered with mud and silt. It must have been swept to this side of the stream by the force of the water, Nancy thought. She shuddered, wondering whether their guide had been swept along with it.

"Do you think the film inside is still good?" Bess asked doubtfully.

"It's possible," Nancy said. "I'll see if I can find a place to get it developed. It'll be a nice surprise for Kim. I see she's used up the whole roll." Nancy slipped the camera into her pocket. Then she and Bess scrambled to catch up with the others, who were already waiting on the trail.

A young man from Search and Rescue was bringing up the end of their group. "Did my friend George contact you?" Nancy asked him. "You reached us pretty quickly."

"We didn't even know there was anyone down there," the man replied. "But we got a very strange report radioed in from one of our helicopters. It seems there was a rainstorm on the north face of the Rincon Mountain Range about ten hours ago."

"You mean that wall of water that just hit here started with a storm ten hours ago?" Nancy asked in disbelief.

The man nodded. "We had rain all last week—enough so that the ground couldn't absorb any more moisture. The water that came rushing down was the rain and melted snow from the top of the range. Took it ten hours to get down to Tanque Verde Falls. About a half mile above you, it met up with that rock that narrows into a chasm and forms the falls. Well, that narrow passage pushed the water up into a twelve-foot wall." He shook his head. "We've seen flash floods before, but never anything like this."

Melina had dropped back to join them. "What about our van?" she demanded. "Our guide had the keys, so now we have no way of getting back."

Nancy frowned. She couldn't believe the way Melina Michaels thought solely of herself. Kim was missing—maybe even swept away by the flood—and Melina's chief concern appeared to be how they would all get back to Spa Solaire.

The young man sighed. "I'll radio the police, and they'll get in touch with someone at the spa. I'm sure they'll send someone right out to pick you up."

"What about George and the others?" Bess

asked as they reached the road. "They went for help, and we don't know where they are."

The young man grinned. "There's really no place for them to go, except the nearest horse ranch. Why don't you all sit tight, and I'll have someone check it out?"

He started back down toward the falls, but Nancy stopped him for one more question. "Do you think our friend Kim will be all right?" she asked.

"I don't know what to tell you," the young man said quietly. "But we'll do our best to find her."

It took a while before George and the others rejoined the group. Soon after someone from the spa who had the keys to the van showed up to drive them all back. No one spoke on the way home. By the time they returned to the spa, it was nearly three in the afternoon.

"I'm going back to the casita to take a nap," George declared with a yawn. "We walked for six miles before we found a phone, which was a much longer hike than any of us had planned. I just want to forget about this whole day."

"Me, too," Bess said. "I'm going to check in at the gym. I think there's a stretching class going on now."

Nancy thought about the roll of film she'd taken out of Kim's camera. "I'll see you guys later," she told her friends. "I have to go take care of something."

Nancy went directly to the office, where she asked the receptionist if she knew of some place nearby where she could have film developed.

"The nearest place is fourteen miles away," the receptionist told her. "However, Solaire has a special service for that. If you leave your film with me, I'll send it out and have the prints back for you tomorrow."

Nancy had her doubts about giving Kim's film to the spa. But she didn't have a car to take the film in herself, and there was no other way for her to get prints made. She handed the receptionist the roll of film and thanked her.

She had just left the office when she noticed Hank Meader and Alain Giraud talking in front of the fountain in the main courtyard. They were an odd pair, Nancy thought. Alain wore a polo shirt and sweats and looked like a model for a sportswear advertisement. Hank stood in dusty jeans, a denim shirt, and boots, looking as if he'd stepped straight out of a western movie.

She was even more surprised when Rhonda Wilkins barged into the middle of their conversation, hands on hips and eyes flashing. The two men looked startled as the heavyset woman began gesturing wildly. "Where were you?" she asked Hank indignantly. "We had a riding lesson scheduled."

Hank tipped his hat to her. "Sorry about that, ma'am. I went to pick up some feed for the horses early this morning, and the fan belt on the pickup broke. Had to hitchhike to the nearest gas station, and then they had to order a replacement. I just got back."

Alain was watching this exchange with obvious amusement when he caught sight of Nancy. "I'm afraid I owe you an apology, too," Alain said, coming over to her. "I'm sorry if I overreacted last night. Is that why you haven't come to the gym yet?"

The truth was that Nancy hadn't even thought about the gym. She'd been too busy worrying about Kim.

"If you come tomorrow, I'll get you started on a personal program," Alain offered.

"Tomorrow," Nancy agreed. She watched him walk off with a confident, athletic stride and wished she hadn't said yes. Something told her that it might be much healthier to avoid Alain Giraud's personal program.

"I've never seen this place so quiet," Bess said the next morning at breakfast.

It was true, Nancy thought. Although the dining hall was full, it was nearly silent. Jacqueline Rozier had just announced that there was still no word on Kim.

"I just wish I knew what Kim's note was about," Nancy said. "I have the awful feeling

51

she's been in danger for a while now, and she was coming to me for help."

"Nan," Bess said hesitantly, "are you sure you aren't trying to create a mystery where there might not be one?"

"Do you really think I'd do that?" Nancy asked, feeling a flash of hurt.

"No," Bess said quickly. "I mean, I don't, but you can't go blaming Kim's disappearance on the spa. It was a freak flash flood. No one could have predicted it, so no one could have set Kim up."

George drained the last of her orange juice. "I agree with Bess about the flood," she said, "but I'm with Nancy as far as thinking there's something strange going on at this place."

Bess stood up. "I'm going to the gym," she announced. "I'll see you two later."

"And there's another strange thing," George said, pointing to Bess's plate. Her breakfast had consisted of a piece of toast, a small serving of fruit salad, orange juice, and another high-energy shake. Bess had left most of her toast and fruit unfinished. "We're being fed less than the average American house cat, and Bess isn't even eating that much," George went on. "I'm really worried about her."

"It's not like Bess," Nancy agreed. "She's always wanted to lose weight, but I've never seen her this serious about it."

"Do you think it's Alain's influence?"

52

George asked. "Bess gets stars in her eyes whenever she mentions his name. Maybe she's trying to impress him."

"Let's join her in the gym and find out," Nancy said.

Twenty minutes later, Nancy and George, dressed in leotards and tights, entered the gym. Bess and five other guests were in the middle of a strenuous aerobics workout, led by Alain. "Higher this time," Alain urged as the class began a third set of leg lifts. "We're going to pick up the pace now. And one, and two . . ."

The aerobics workout soon ended, but Bess remained in the gym. The other four women filed past Nancy on their way to the locker room. Her face flushed, and breathing hard, Bess headed straight to one of the weight machines. Alain helped her adjust the settings, and within minutes Bess was hard at work, this time building her biceps.

"This is unbelievable," George murmured. "She's really overdoing it. Do you think we should say something to her?"

"Maybe," Nancy replied. "But I doubt she'll listen to us."

Alain caught sight of the two girls and came over to greet them. "I'm glad you're here for your first workout."

"Oh, so am I," Nancy said, wondering if Alain might be a good source of information about Solaire. She remembered something she'd read in one of the brochures. "The Roziers had another spa before this one," she said, as they walked across the room toward the first set of machines. "Did you work there as well?"

"No," Alain answered with a smile. "The previous Solaire was on the island of St. Martin, I believe. I'm afraid I've never been to the Caribbean."

He turned as another guest entered the gym, a pink towel slung around her neck. "Whitney," he called out, "you can go up to sixty pounds today." The young woman nodded and began adjusting the weights on one of the weight machines.

"Now," Alain said, turning back to Nancy and George, "that's enough chatting. Time to go to work."

Alain started Nancy on the treadmill and George on the grueling Stairmaster. Nancy began walking, noting that Alain had chosen a reasonable pace for her—not too fast and not too slow.

"Are you from France, like the Roziers?" she asked him when he came to check on her.

"Quebec, Canada," he replied, increasing her pace slightly. "The Roziers prefer that their staff be fluent in French."

"Why is that?" Nancy pressed.

Instead of answering, Alain increased the

pace on the treadmill until Nancy was puffing too hard to talk. Then he headed off to check on Bess.

Panting, Nancy reached out and quickly reset the machine. As the treadmill gradually slowed, she became aware of a sound beyond her own rapid breathing. Whitney was sitting on the weight machine's bench, clutching her left shoulder and moaning softly. "My arm," she sobbed. "I think it's broken!"

6

No Pain, No Gain

Nancy, George, and Alain all reached the stricken guest at the same time. "What happened?" Alain demanded.

Whitney nodded toward a cable that had snapped, sending a stack of flat weights to the floor. "My arm," she sobbed. "When the cable broke, it yanked my shoulder real hard." She winced in pain. "I think something broke."

"I'll get Dr. Benay," George offered.

"Try not to move," Alain told Whitney, his voice soothing. "How did the cable snap?" he added in a bewildered tone.

"This cable didn't fray and snap," Nancy said, examining one neatly broken end of the metal cord. "Someone cut right through it."

"That's impossible," Alain said, frowning. "I check the equipment every morning and—"

Just then, brisk footsteps sounded on the

hardwood floor as Dr. Benay rushed across the gym. "Let me see the patient, please." She knelt beside Whitney, carefully examined her, and then made a sling to support the injured arm with an elastic bandage she took from her pocket. "I think you may have pulled a ligament," she said at last. "Still, I want to take some X-rays to be sure."

Whitney stopped sobbing as soon as Dr. Benay had put on the sling. But she was still white-faced with pain as she stood up. "I'll be calling my lawyer," she informed Alain icily. "The Roziers advertise Solaire as the finest spa in the country, but they don't even check to make sure their equipment is safe. They won't get away with this."

"Please," Alain said. "I checked that machine this morning. There was nothing wrong with it. I'm sure it was an accident."

"Then you'll have a chance to explain that in court," Whitney replied as she left the gym.

"How can you call this an accident?" George demanded of the trainer.

"Look at the cable," Nancy added. "It didn't just wear out. Someone cut through it."

"No one would tamper with our equipment," Alain snapped. "It must have been faulty. And this whole thing is none of your business. I suggest that you two get back to work, like Bess."

"No thanks," George said quietly. "I don't

think I want to take my personal program quite that seriously."

For the first time, Nancy realized that, if Bess had noticed Whitney's accident, she hadn't bothered to stop and see whether Whitney was all right. Bess was still on the other side of the room, working away on her weight machine. She looked driven—and exhausted.

"I'm going back to the casita," George said.

"Me, too," Nancy said. She walked over to Bess. "George and I are going back to the room now. Want to come?"

"Can't," Bess huffed. "I've got to stretch out after this. So my muscles stay long and supple."

Nancy sighed. "Okay, Bess. We'll see you later."

"What is wrong with Alain?" George said the minute she and Nancy were back in their room. "How can he pretend that what happened to Whitney was just an accident?"

Nancy frowned. "I can't think on an empty stomach anymore." Then she grinned at her friend, went to her suitcase, and took out two chocolate bars. She held one out to George. "My secret spa survival kit. Don't tell Alain." She unwrapped the candy bar and took a satisfying bite. "Mmmm. And as for Alain— he'd *have* to pretend the severed cable was an

58

accident if he were responsible for it in the first place."

"I don't know," George said reluctantly. "Alain may have acted like a jerk, but I can't believe he'd sabotage the gym. It's too obvious. He'd get fired instantly." She munched on the candy bar. "This chocolate tastes great, by the way."

"Alain certainly is suspicious," Nancy mused. "He turns on the charm one minute, then acts as if he'll bite your head off the next. I don't trust that guy at all."

"Bess does," George said ruefully.

As if on cue, the door opened and a tired-looking Bess trudged into the room. "Bess does what?" she asked. "Aerobics? Weights? Stretching? Dieting?" She collapsed onto one of the chairs. "Bess does them all, and she may never move again."

"You really look beat," Nancy said sympathetically.

"I am," Bess said. She leaned forward, her eyes narrowing. "Is that chocolate, or am I hallucinating?"

"It's chocolate," Nancy told her. "Do you want some?"

Bess shut her eyes. "I didn't see a candy bar, and I don't smell it. It's a figment of my imagination."

"Bess, you're losing it," George said. When her cousin didn't reply, she added gently, "You

59

know, you might want to take things slower and build up to all this exercise gradually. It'd be a lot easier on your body."

Bess opened one eye. "I'm only going to be here a week. Besides, I've already lost exactly one point two pounds. I can't stop now. You know what they say—no pain, no gain."

"Did Alain say that?" Nancy asked.

"Everyone says it," Bess replied. "It's true."

George stood up, putting her hands on her hips. "I am so tired of everyone in sports saying 'No pain, no gain,' as if it were some law! The truth is, you can get stronger and more limber and into better shape without hurting yourself."

"George, you're a natural athlete," Bess pointed out. "You can do a seven-minute mile without breathing hard. You've probably never had an ounce of fat on your body in your entire life. You don't have to sweat to look great."

"Bess, I think you look fine the way you are," Nancy said truthfully.

"You're just saying that because you're my friend," Bess replied. She stood up and stretched. "I need a shower."

George shook her head as the sound of running water came on. "I believe in working out," she said, "but this is ridiculous."

"Well, we are only here for a week," Nancy reminded her. "I don't think Bess will keep up this pace once we're back in River Heights. But I don't like the idea of Bess—or anyone—

working out in a place where so many things are going wrong. Someone's sabotaging Solaire, and the Roziers and their staff are doing everything possible to pretend it isn't happening."

"Of course they are," George said. "It wouldn't exactly help their reputation if people knew what was going on."

"But what *is* going on?" Nancy wondered aloud. "And why? Are the Roziers being sabotaged by a dissatisfied client? Or maybe by an angry employee—someone they fired?"

"Or one of Jacqueline's ex-boyfriends," George guessed. "It's impossible to tell."

Nancy sighed. "I still think Kim had the key to the whole story. Where do you suppose she is right now? I hope she's okay."

Bess emerged from the shower and began changing into a T-shirt, sweatpants, and sneakers.

"You're not going back into the gym, are you?" George asked her cousin.

"No, I just like the way workout clothes look," Bess said, sounding more like her old self. "They make me feel athletic, even if I'm really not." She glanced at the spa schedule that lay on the table. "Why don't we all go for our facials this afternoon?" she suggested.

"Sounds good to me," Nancy said. "Lunch first, and then the salon."

* * *

Nancy lay back on a reclining chair, every inch of her body cushioned and relaxed. Soft music was filtering down from the loudspeakers, her eyes were closed, and a woman named Yvette was applying a thick layer of cool green mud to her face. It felt fantastic.

Bess lay on the chair beside Nancy. "I can just feel all my pores breathing," she murmured. "My skin is improving every second."

"You've always had great skin," George reminded her.

"Solaire mineral mud is good for everyone," Yvette said diplomatically.

Nancy opened her eyes as she heard the door to the salon open. Melina Michaels hesitated a moment, then walked in. Nancy hadn't really spoken to Melina since yesterday's hike. Melina had acted so selfishly then that Nancy hadn't planned to talk to her at all. But at dinner last night and at breakfast and lunch earlier in the day, she noticed that Melina always sat alone. And for some reason Nancy felt sorry for her. What Melina probably needed, she decided, was a good friend.

"Hi, Melina," she said in a friendly tone. "Are you here for your mud treatment?"

"I don't think so," Melina replied, "I just wanted to see what was going on in here."

"The treatment is fabulous," Bess assured her. "Now I know why Jacqueline has such perfect skin."

62

"You don't really think Jacqueline Rozier uses that stuff, do you?" Melina scoffed.

"Of course Jacqueline uses Solaire products," Yvette said quickly. "If you sit in that chair over there on the right, I'll be with you in a moment."

"No thanks. What if you just give me some of that stuff in a jar, and I'll put it on in my room?" Melina countered.

Nancy frowned. Melina seemed to enjoy making things difficult for people whenever possible.

"It's not just the mud," Yvette explained. "There is a cleaning solution to remove it, a gentle astringent and moisturizer afterward, and a special cream to be applied around the eyes. It's best if you let me take you through the routine the first time."

"It does feel great," George said with a sigh.

Melina hesitated a moment, then lay down in the chair on the right. "Okay, okay," she told Yvette. But minutes later, when Yvette brought over the ceramic bowl filled with mineral mud, Melina sat bolt upright. "Don't touch me," she hissed, and then fled from the salon.

"What was all *that* about?" George asked.

"I don't know," Yvette said.

Me neither, Nancy thought. But it's definitely one more strange incident at Solaire to add to the list.

* * *

Nancy, Bess, and George had just left the salon when they saw the woman who worked at the office desk hurrying toward them.

"Ms. Drew," she said, "your photographs just came back. Would you like to pick them up?"

"Definitely," Nancy replied.

She and Bess and George followed the woman back to the office, where the woman handed Nancy a sealed paper envelope. "Hope they turned out well," the woman said with a smile.

"Thanks," Nancy said. "I can't wait to look at them." But she made herself wait until she and her friends were safely back in their casita.

The first half of Kim's roll was all desert shots—a majestic saguaro cactus, the Catalina Mountains at sunset, a stand of wildflowers, a coyote crossing a dirt road.

"Here are the ones from the hike," Nancy said, holding up one of the group shots. Then she frowned. "This is interesting," she murmured, looking at the photograph Bess had taken of her and Kim. "Check out what's behind Kim," Nancy said, handing the photo to George. What was behind Kim was the opposite shore of Tanque Verde Creek—the sloping white rock where Nancy had last seen Kim seconds before the flood hit.

"You mean the rock?" George asked.

"I mean this bit of brown and blue plaid *on* the rock," Nancy answered, pointing to a small

64

corner of plaid at the very edge of the picture. "It looks like it could be the elbow of someone wearing a plaid shirt. Was anyone in our group wearing plaid that day?"

George and Bess both thought for a moment before shaking their heads.

"But we were the only ones down there," Bess said.

"We *thought* we were," Nancy said, trying to ignore a creeping feeling of dread. "But what if someone else was there all along? And what if the floodwaters didn't get Kim? What if our mystery person did?"

7

Spies in the Night

George sat cross-legged on the bed, her dark eyes disbelieving. "Let me get this straight," she said slowly. "You're saying Kim Foster was *kidnapped?*"

"I'm not sure," Nancy admitted. "There's a good chance she was swept downstream by the flood. But Search and Rescue still hasn't found any trace of her."

"But who would have kidnapped Kim?" Bess asked. "And why?"

"Kim was trying to give me some sort of information about Solaire," Nancy said slowly. "I think someone wanted to make sure she never told anyone anything."

Bess ran a brush through her straw-colored hair. "I can't believe someone from the spa would get involved in a kidnapping," she said. "That's crazy!"

"Maybe," Nancy agreed. "But what if Alain had been at the falls at the same time we were?"

"Alain doesn't wear anything like that shirt," Bess said. "He usually wears workout clothes."

"Actually, I haven't seen anyone here wearing a flannel shirt," George admitted. "The sun's been too hot. Just about everyone wears T-shirts or polo shirts or tank tops."

"That's true," Nancy said with a sigh. "If there *was* another person down at the falls, it could have been someone totally unconnected to Solaire. Which makes this even more of a mystery," she added.

"Maybe we should go to the police," George suggested.

"The police already know about Kim's disappearance," Nancy reminded her. "Jacqueline said they've been working with the Search and Rescue team, looking for her."

"But they don't know what's going on here at the spa," George pointed out.

"Neither do we," Nancy said glumly. "And we have no real evidence whatsoever. I need more information before I can go to them."

Later that afternoon, the three girls sat near the edge of the pool, talking. The day was getting cooler, and they were the last guests remaining by the water.

"It's just too beautiful to go indoors," Bess

said contentedly. "I'm even thinking I need some outdoor exercise. Maybe I'll sign up for a riding lesson tomorrow."

"Oh!" Nancy exclaimed suddenly.

"Oh, what?" George asked.

"Hank Meader, that's what."

Bess dangled one leg in the cool water. "What about him?"

"Yesterday, after we got back from the falls, I saw Hank by the fountain, talking to Alain," Nancy explained. "Anyway, Rhonda Wilkins came up to him, all upset because she'd scheduled a riding lesson with him, and he'd missed it. Hank told her it was because he'd been out buying horse feed that morning, and the fan belt on his pickup truck broke."

"So?" George asked.

"So Hank wasn't where he was supposed to be yesterday afternoon. Maybe he wasn't buying horse feed, either," Nancy said. "Maybe he was really at Tanque Verde Falls."

Bess applied more sun block and took a drink of bottled water. "I don't know, Nan," she said doubtfully. "That sounds a little farfetched to me. Why don't you believe Hank's story?"

"It's just a hunch," Nancy admitted with a smile. "To tell you the truth, this theory does sound a little crazy, even to me."

"Was Hank wearing a plaid shirt?" George asked.

68

Nancy shook her head. "No, blue denim. But it *was* a long-sleeved shirt, and Hank dresses kind of like a cowboy. He's definitely the type who'd own a plaid shirt. He could have been down at the falls, and then changed before coming back here."

George stretched out on one of the lounges. "Not that I understand why Hank Meader would want to kidnap Kim, or how he could have been standing there and escaped the flood . . . but how do we find out if he owns a blue and brown plaid shirt?"

"Well, I'm pretty sure he lives on the grounds of the spa," Nancy said. "There's a small adobe house that must have been part of the original ranch, about a hundred yards behind the stables. I've seen Hank go into it."

"What if it's the tack room?" George asked.

"No one puts a tack room that far away from the stables," Nancy said. "It's got to be Hank's house. And I'd love to have a look inside."

Bess scrunched her eyes shut tight. "Why do I have this feeling that I'm going to help you break into someone's house?"

Nancy grinned. "You don't actually have to help me break in, Bess. All you have to do is distract Hank."

Dinner had just ended later that evening, and the setting sun had turned the western horizon into a blazing streak of crimson. Nancy, Bess, and George left Solaire's dining room and headed for the stables.

"Let's go over the plan one more time," Nancy said.

"Okay. I go into the stables and ask Hank if he'll show me around," Bess began. "I tell him I want to go riding tomorrow, and that I'd feel a lot better about it if I could see the horses first. Then I'll take a long time at each stall—asking lots of questions and talking to the horses and stuff." Bess reached into her pocket and pulled out a fistful of carrot sticks she'd taken from the salad bar. "See? I even came prepared."

"And I'm the lookout," George continued. "I'll hide somewhere near the door of the stables. As soon as Hank even hints that he might leave, I'll signal you in the house." She paused. "What kind of signal should I use?"

"Um—how about throwing some dirt at one of the windows?" Nancy suggested. "I'll hear that."

"Right," George said.

Nancy took a deep breath as she considered her own part in the plan. "And I'm going to break into Hank Meader's house and search for the shirt." She shook her head. "If my dad, the lawyer, only knew . . ."

Bess giggled nervously. "This sounds like a spy movie."

"We are spying," Nancy admitted as the stable building came into view. "But it's for a good cause. We have to find out what happened to Kim."

Dusk was falling now. The wooden stables were lit from inside, and the scents of hay and horses filled the air.

Nancy headed off to the right, planning to circle back toward Hank's house.

"Wish me luck," Bess called softly.

"Good luck," Nancy whispered, "to all of us." She walked as quietly as she could, praying that Hank didn't have a dog or some sort of burglar alarm. At least none of the windows in the stables faced the house. Hank couldn't possibly see her.

The house was smaller and older than Nancy had realized. Its adobe walls were cracked from years in the sun, and the inside was completely dark. For a moment, Nancy wondered if anyone actually did live there.

Calmly, Nancy walked up to the thick wooden door and knocked, just in case someone other than Hank lived there. When no one answered, Nancy tried the doorknob. Unsurprisingly, it was locked. I guess I'll have to break in after all, she thought.

Carefully, she walked around the side of the house. The windows weren't that far from the ground. She could probably boost herself up onto one of the thick wooden ledges, but then how would she actually get the window open?

At the back of the house, Nancy found her

answer. The back window was open. The sky was growing darker by the minute, and Nancy knew she had no time to lose. She jumped up onto the thick wooden ledge, then lowered herself feet first through the open window.

Her feet came down and Nancy heard the sound of something breaking. She froze, terrified. What had she broken? Had someone heard her?

Inside, the house was silent.

Taking a deep breath, Nancy turned on her flashlight and found a broken terra-cotta planter on the floor.

Nice move, Drew, she told herself, as she swept up the broken pieces and hid them deep in the garbage can.

Using her flashlight, Nancy checked out the tiny living room, bedroom, and kitchen. In the bedroom closet, she found plenty of long-sleeved shirts, even a few that were plaid, but none of the patterns matched the one in the photograph.

Maybe Bess was right, Nancy thought as she got ready to climb back out of the kitchen window. Maybe my theory was crazy. Then she realized there was one room she still hadn't checked: the bathroom.

Shining her flashlight ahead of her, Nancy entered the narrow bathroom. Lying in a heap on the tile floor was a muddy plaid shirt. Nancy's hand shook with excitement as she took the photograph from her pocket and held it against the sleeve of the shirt. It was a perfect match.

Now what? she wondered. It'd be bad enough if Hank noticed he was missing a planter. She couldn't risk taking the shirt for evidence.

Nancy made one more check through the small house, searching for something else that might lead her to Kim. This time, a photograph on top of the dresser in the bedroom caught her eye. The photograph showed a lovely young woman standing beside a white horse, holding a trophy. Could this be Hank's daughter? Nancy wondered.

She turned over the picture. The cardboard backing was slightly pulled down. Beneath it, Nancy could see what looked like newsprint. Curious, she slipped the photograph from its frame. A yellowed newspaper clipping fell out and fluttered to the floor.

Nancy carefully unfolded the brittle piece of paper. It was a newspaper article, and its headline read: Local Woman, 20, Blinded by Tainted Cosmetics. Beneath the headline was the same picture of the girl with the horse.

Nancy's heart skipped a beat as she went on to read about Heather Sinclair, a promising equestrian from Arizona. She'd been studying in Paris and was blinded by a French-manufactured mascara. The cosmetics company, Jeunesse, paid Ms. Sinclair's hospital bills but vanished before paying the damages they'd agreed to. The girl's father, Henry Sinclair, was being forced to sell his ranch to pay for legal fees to try and bring the Jeunesse company to justice.

Henry Sinclair, Nancy mused. Could he possibly be the same man as Hank Meader? There was no way of telling. How long ago did this happen? Nancy checked for a date, but the article had been clipped from the middle of a page.

A sudden sound against the bedroom window made her jump. It was George's signal— Hank was coming! Moving swiftly, Nancy slipped the article back into the frame and set the picture back on top of the dresser. Then she made her way back to the kitchen.

"Please stall him, Bess," Nancy murmured as she climbed onto the window ledge and lowered herself to the ground.

George was waiting for her, and she whispered to Nancy to hurry. The girls glanced toward the barn, but they didn't see Hank coming.

Suddenly Nancy heard footsteps from around the corner of the house. She grabbed George's arm, and the two of them sprinted off in the other direction, not daring to look back.

* * *

When the girls had finally let themselves into the room, Nancy's heart was still pounding.

"That was a close one," Nancy said, collapsing into a chair.

"Are you okay?" George asked at once. Even George was winded.

"Fine," Nancy told her. "I'll explain everything I found in a minute, but first I need to make a call."

Nancy hurried to the bedside phone and dialed her father's number. "Hi, Dad," she said when Carson Drew answered the phone. "Yes, we're all fine. I was wondering if you could do a little research for me. I need to know anything you can find out about a French cosmetics company called Jeunesse and an American girl from Tucson named Heather Sinclair, who was blinded by one of their products. Also anything you can find on Jacqueline and Laurent Rozier."

"What was that all about?" Bess asked after Nancy had chatted with her dad for a few minutes and hung up the phone.

Nancy told her friends what she'd found in Hank Meader's cottage. "I'm not sure why he was at the falls that day," she said. "And I don't know for certain that he has Kim—but it seems very possible."

George pulled a pillow from her bed and

75

stretched out on the rug. "So what's his connection to the girl in the photograph?" she asked.

"I'm not sure," Nancy replied, "but I intend to find out."

"Well, I don't know why you're checking out the Roziers," Bess said, sounding upset. "I'm sure they didn't have anything to do with it."

Nancy sighed, not wanting to get into an argument with Bess. Then her eyes widened in panic. "I can't believe it," she said. "It's gone!"

"What is?" George asked, frowning.

"My silver bracelet. The one Ned gave me. It says, 'To Nancy, with love' on the inside."

"Are you sure you didn't just leave it somewhere?" Bess asked.

"Positive," Nancy said, her heart sinking. "I know I had it on before I went into Hank's house. And now it's gone."

The three girls jumped as someone pounded on their door. Putting a finger to her lips, Nancy went to open it. What she saw made her heart start racing all over again.

Framed in the dark doorway was Hank Meader, a menacing scowl on his face.

8

Run for Your Life

Nancy stared into Hank Meader's angry face and felt herself start to tremble. He knows I broke into his house, she thought. How am I ever going to talk my way out of this one?

"The Roziers want to see the three of you in the office," Hank said. "Pronto!"

"Wh-what?" Nancy stammered. Was he telling the truth, or was this some kind of ruse to get them out of the casita?

"I said, they want to see you in the office," Hank repeated. "Look," he went on impatiently, "I've got a mare about to foal in the stables. I don't have all night to run errands. Do you think you three could move it?"

"He does have a mare about to foal," Bess said quickly. "Her name's Bonita and—"

"All right," Nancy said, "we'll come with

77

you." Maybe Hank *was* telling the truth, but why had the Roziers summoned them?

Silently, Hank led the way toward the main complex. By night the fountain was lit, throwing a soft cascade of silver water under the moonlight.

The three girls entered the office and found both Jacqueline and Laurent waiting for them. "*Merci*, Hank," Jacqueline said. "You may go now."

Hank tipped his hat and left, leaving Nancy more curious than ever. Did the Roziers know the girls had been spying? Were she and Bess and George about to be thrown out of Solaire?

"I summoned you because we have received word from Kim Foster," Jacqueline began. "I have already told the staff the news, and I am speaking to the other guests in the morning, but I know how particularly concerned you three have been."

"Did Search and Rescue find her?" George asked eagerly.

"No, but there was no need," Jacqueline explained. "We received this from her today." She held out a typed letter to Nancy, who read the letter aloud to her friends.

"Dear Jacqueline and Laurent,
    I just wanted to let you know that I am fine. I was swept downstream in the flood,

78

but I managed to make it to safety. Still, nearly drowning is an upsetting experience—
especially for a 'wilderness expert.' I need
some time to think things through, so I will not
be returning to Solaire. I'm going to spend the
next few weeks in Phoenix, visiting museums
and taking in the sights.

   I'd appreciate it if you could hold my mail
and things until I return.

   All the best,

Kim Foster"

Nancy reread the letter silently. Something
about it didn't sound right. "Are you sure that's
Kim's signature?" she asked the Roziers.

"Of course," Laurent said. "In fact, I will
prove it to you." He went over to a wooden
filing cabinet, pulled out a typed form, and
handed it to Nancy. It was Kim's original job
application. The signature was identical to the
one on the letter.

"So she's really all right," Bess said, smiling.

"She's fine," Jacqueline said, putting the
application away. "We will miss her, of course,
and it was quite irresponsible of her to walk out
on us, but we are very relieved that she is all
right. Now, you girls must return to your casita
and get a good night's rest. Alain is waiting
outside to walk you back to your room."

Why do I feel as if I've just been conned?

Nancy wondered. "Jacqueline," she said impulsively, "does the name Jeunesse mean anything to you?"

"Of course. It's a French word that means youth," Jacqueline replied.

"I meant Jeunesse cosmetics," Nancy said. "Have you ever heard of them, maybe while you were living in Paris?"

Jacqueline gave a soft laugh. "When I lived in Paris, I was a model. I used every cosmetic on the market. I never distinguished one brand from the other. All I remember is that the makeup artists took entirely too long to get me ready for the cameras."

"Laurent," Nancy asked, "have *you* ever heard of Jeunesse cosmetics?"

"I'm afraid not," he replied, smoothly taking Nancy by the arm and escorting her to the door. "Good night, mademoiselles."

Nancy's level of frustration rose another notch when she found Alain and his guard dog waiting outside the door.

"*Bon soir*, Alain," Bess greeted him.

"*Bon soir*," he replied, smiling.

"Since when did Bess learn to speak French?" George whispered to Nancy.

Nancy shrugged and turned her attention to Alain. "We appreciate the escort," she said, "but we can find our way back to the casita on our own."

"I'm sure you can," Alain replied. "However, Solaire believes in protecting its guests at all times."

"And making them feel like prisoners," George muttered as the four of them began walking toward the casita. "Look." She pointed to several shadowy figures in the distance. "There are three other staff members patrolling the grounds with dogs. Are you guys expecting an armed invasion?"

"These are normal security measures," Alain said. "Please don't be alarmed. I assure you, they are for your own good."

Alain, Nancy thought, was about as informative and truthful as Laurent. Still, since he insisted on walking them back to the casita, she might as well try to get some information. "So, how is Whitney?" she asked.

"Whitney pulled a shoulder ligament," Alain replied. "She may be a bit uncomfortable for a while, but Dr. Benay says her arm should heal perfectly. I believe Whitney's decided to return home tomorrow." He shrugged as they reached the casita. "It was a most unfortunate accident."

"Except that it wasn't an accident," Nancy said.

Alain's eyes met hers with something that might have been respect, but his words were a warning. "I would suggest, Ms. Drew," he said softly, "that you keep your opinions to yourself."

81

They entered the room, and George shut the door on Alain with a thump.

"George," Bess said, "you don't have to be so rude."

"*Me?*" George asked. "Alain practically threatens Nancy and you're calling me rude?"

"It wasn't a threat," Bess insisted.

"Let's not argue about Alain right now," Nancy said. "There's a phone call I have to make before I forget the number."

She took the phone from the bedside table and dialed the number she'd memorized from Kim's employment application. On the other end of the line, an answering machine came on, telling Nancy she'd reached the Foster residence. Nancy sighed and left her number, hoping Kim's family would call back.

The phone rang a few hours later, just as the girls were dropping off to sleep. "Mrs. Foster?" Nancy asked eagerly.

"No," said a dry voice at the other end of the line. "It's your father. Will that do?"

"Dad!" Nancy exclaimed. "I can't believe you're getting back to me so soon."

"Well, it sounded pretty urgent," Carson Drew said. "So I called a few friends, here and in Paris, and got some information. First, I checked out the Roziers. The two of them ran a very exclusive spa on the island of St. Martin, also called Spa Solaire. That's apparently where Laurent developed his line of cosmetics."

"That's pretty much what I read in the Solaire brochures," Nancy said with a sigh. "Did you find any information on what they were doing before St. Martin?"

Her father gave a soft laugh. "Now, that's rather interesting. About five years before the Roziers showed up in St. Martin, Jacqueline officially retired as one of Paris's leading fashion models. She wasn't married to Laurent then. She was simply known as Jacqueline. And then, it seems, she dropped off the face of the planet. There's no more information about her until she showed up in St. Martin with Laurent three years ago, purchased an old resort, and opened the first Solaire."

"What about Laurent?" Nancy asked.

"Again, nothing," Carson Drew replied. "All I found was a marriage certificate."

"And Heather Sinclair?"

"Five years ago, she and several others sued Jeunesse. Heather had developed a severe eye infection after using their mascara, and she eventually went blind. Another American, a young model who was working in Paris, had such a severe allergic reaction to the Jeunesse cold cream that it left her skin permanently scarred. Her career was ruined. Jeunesse paid the immediate medical costs and agreed to a hefty settlement. But the settlement was never paid."

"Why not?" Nancy asked, her curiosity growing.

"Well, one day there was a Jeunesse and the next day, the company was gone. The office was empty, the bank accounts were closed, and the staff was gone."

"Who was the owner?" Nancy asked.

"A chemist named Pierre Dennon, who also pulled a disappearing act," Carson Drew replied. "His car went off a cliff and exploded. No one ever found the body."

"Dad," Nancy said slowly, "do you think Pierre Dennon could be Laurent Rozier?"

"I was wondering the same thing," her father said.

Nancy had one more question. "And what happened to Heather Sinclair?"

"Another mystery," Carson Drew answered. "She returned to the States, but her father, Henry, had sold his ranch. There's no other record of them in Arizona. I'll have to keep working on it."

"Thanks for all your help, Dad," Nancy said. "I'll let you know if I come up with anything."

She placed the phone receiver back on the hook and glanced over at Bess and George. Both of her friends were sound asleep. She'd have to wait until morning to fill them in on the latest news. Maybe that was just as well. It was going to take her a while to put all of the pieces together.

Nancy woke up the next morning to find Bess already dressed in her workout clothes, doing leg lifts on the floor. Bess was definitely losing weight, Nancy saw, but there were dark shadows under her friend's eyes. For someone who'd just gotten up, Bess looked exhausted. "Isn't it a little early for exercise?" Nancy asked.

George opened one eye. "It definitely is."

"There's no time to waste," Bess said. "Alain gave me all these exercises for toning and calorie-burning. I won't lose weight unless I do them."

Nancy got out of bed and searched for her clothes. "But you've got a whole day of exercise scheduled already," she said to Bess. "Aren't you overdoing all of this?"

"Alain says, 'Listen to your body. It always knows,'" Bess quoted. "And what my body knows right now is that it can't wait to be thin. All this exercise feels fantastic!"

George sat up and threw her pillow at Bess. "Come on, Bess. Give it up."

Bess raised her chin. "You're just jealous, because for once I'm working out harder than you are!"

George sighed and climbed out of bed. "Okay, Bess, maybe you're right. I might as

85

well join you. They're going to rename this place 'Spa Kill-aire.' "

An hour later, after another minuscule breakfast, the three girls reported to the gym, where a small group had already gathered.

"Good morning, everyone," Alain said. "We're going to start outside today, with a little run around the grounds."

"A *little* run?" echoed one of the guests. "These grounds cover more than a hundred acres."

Rhonda Wilkins was already jogging in place. She looked even more exhausted than Bess, Nancy thought.

"Let's go!" Alain barked, and set off at a brisk pace.

Nancy and the others all fell into place behind the trainer. It actually felt good to be running outside, Nancy thought. The morning air was still cool, the birds were calling, and the cacti were bright green against the perfectly clear sky. Alain led the guests around the main complex, over to the tennis courts, back around the stables and Hank's house, and then down the main road to the gate.

Nancy found herself growing winded as they approached the two tall wooden posts and the sign that swung between them. Bess had dropped back a while ago, but George was still running easily at the head of the pack. Nancy watched as her friend widened the gap between herself and the others.

Alain signaled to George as she loped beneath the gate. She stopped and waited for the rest of the pack, her hands on her knees.

Nancy would have loved to have stopped as well. She was incredibly thirsty, and each step was getting harder. But her pride wouldn't let her give up. She knew she had to make it through the gate. She gritted her teeth as Melina Michaels passed her from behind, then raced under the gate. I must be really slow, Nancy thought. Melina wasn't exactly the most motivated person.

Nancy neared the gate, panting so loudly that she was sure they could hear her in Texas. Alain stood on the other side, holding a stopwatch and frowning. "Come on!" he called to Nancy. "Pick up the pace now, and go for a sprint!"

The request was so unreasonable that Nancy felt her temper rise. Fortunately, with her anger came a burst of energy. Nancy dashed beneath the gate, then halted abruptly as she saw Melina's face take on an expression of horror. Seconds later, she heard a deafening crash and a woman's scream.

9

Alive and Unwell

Nancy spun around. The heavy wooden Solaire sign had crashed to the ground, barely missing her and Rhonda Wilkins, who was only a few feet behind Nancy. Rhonda stood on the other side of the gate, her hands over her mouth, her eyes wide with fear. She was the one who'd screamed.

"You'd better sit down for a minute," Alain said, taking Rhonda by the arm and gently leading the heavy woman to a boulder on the side of the road. "You're hyperventilating. Try to control your breathing. Slow it down."

Nancy bent down to examine the fallen wooden sign. A crosspiece had hung from the two wooden posts, and the Solaire sign had been attached to the crosspiece by rawhide strips. Maybe the sign fell because the rawhide wore out, Nancy thought.

88

Then she examined the sign more closely, and a shiver ran through her. Both strips of rawhide had been sliced halfway through, allowing the weight of the sign to tear the rest of the way through the rawhide. It looked a lot like the work of whoever had sabotaged the weight machine.

Nancy glanced up at Alain, who was still trying to calm Rhonda. "I think you ought to take a look at this," Nancy called to the trainer.

A few minutes later, he came over and examined the rawhide strips and the fallen sign.

"Are you going to tell me this was an accident, too?" Nancy asked.

"I—I—" Alain stammered.

"What is going on here?" Melina shrieked. "First Whitney is hurt, and now this! Were you trying to kill all of us? You deliberately led us through this gate."

"That's because it's exactly one and a half miles from the gym," Alain said, regaining his composure. "We always take this route on the first run. And nothing like this has ever happened."

"Except for the weight machine," George reminded him.

Alain glared at her. Then his face went red as he saw a silver Mercedes approaching. "Wonderful," he muttered. "Just what I need now—a visit from Jacqueline."

A few moments later, Jacqueline emerged

from the Mercedes. "What has happened to the sign?" she asked, sounding nearly hysterical. "How is anyone supposed to get in or out of the spa with a sign lying in the middle of the road?"

Alain began what seemed to be a lengthy explanation in French.

Jacqueline cut him off angrily and called Hank Meader from her car phone. Nancy heard her ask Hank to bring the truck and remove the sign. Then she turned and addressed her guests. "I must ask your forgiveness. I do not know how this could have happened. I am just so glad that no one was hurt. If you will please follow Alain back to the gym, we will see that nothing like this happens again."

"I don't believe you," Melina said angrily. "Yesterday it was an accident in the gym, today there's another one out here. Just how many of these near-disasters do you expect us to risk? Solaire isn't safe, and you know it!"

"That's not true," Jacqueline said, but Nancy noticed that the woman's voice was shaking slightly.

Melina stalked off toward the gym, and most of the others followed. Only Nancy, Bess, and George remained with Jacqueline.

"Jacqueline," Nancy said, "this was no accident. Did you see how the rawhide strips were cut?"

Jacqueline nodded, brushing a silver-blond strand of hair away from her face.

"Who would do something like this to you?" Nancy asked.

"I don't know," Jacqueline said, her eyes still fixed on the sign. "We have never had enemies in the past. Perhaps someone is jealous of our success."

Jacqueline's explanation didn't sound very convincing to Nancy. "Can you think of anyone specific?"

Jacqueline shook her head. "No one." She looked up. "Thank you for your concern. Now, I'm afraid I must go." Before Nancy could stop her, the Frenchwoman got into her Mercedes, drove around the sign, and sped away from the grounds.

"Poor Jacqueline," Bess said. "I think this was a terrible shock to her."

"I don't," Nancy said. "I think she knows exactly what's going on, and she's terrified to admit it."

Later that afternoon, Nancy, Bess, and George were changing into swimsuits back in the casita when the phone rang. "I'll get it," Nancy called.

"Ms. Drew?" said an unfamiliar voice. "This is Ruth Foster. You left a message for me."

"Yes," Nancy said. "Your daughter Kim sent a letter to the Roziers yesterday, and I was wondering if you'd heard from her as well."

"As a matter of fact, she called yesterday morning," Kim's mother answered. "I was so relieved to hear her voice!"

"Where did she call from?" Nancy asked curiously.

"Tucson, I suppose," Mrs. Foster replied. "I live about sixty miles south of the city. Kim told me she'd been caught in the flood, but was washed onto dry land. The flood left her pretty bruised, and it took her a while to get back to civilization. Thank goodness she's so at home in the desert."

"Did Kim say where she was going?" Nancy asked.

"No. But she told me she'd quit her job at the spa because she needed some time off."

"I guess she was anxious to get to Phoenix," Nancy said. "That's what she wrote in her letter."

"Phoenix?" Mrs. Foster echoed. "Are you sure?"

"That's what her letter said," Nancy said.

"But my daughter can't stand Phoenix," Mrs. Foster said. "She calls it Congestion City."

"Her letter said she wanted to see the museums," Nancy explained.

"Museums?" Now Mrs. Foster's voice was edged with astonishment. "I haven't been able to get that girl inside a museum since she was ten. Kim's always been too restless to spend much time indoors. She's not happy unless she's hiking up a mountain or camping under the stars. . . . Museums! Why, surviving that flood must have changed her whole way of thinking. I just don't understand it."

Nancy chatted with Mrs. Foster for a while longer. Then she hung up and sat silently on the edge of the bed, trying to make sense of what she'd just learned.

"What is it, Nan?" Bess asked. "You've got a strange look on your face."

"Well, the good news is that Kim's alive," Nancy answered. "At least, she was yesterday morning when she called her mother. But her mom was very surprised to hear that Kim wanted to go to Phoenix and see museums. Mrs. Foster said that sounded completely out of character for her daughter."

"Maybe Kim decided she needed some culture," Bess said optimistically.

"Or maybe," Nancy said slowly, "someone forced Kim to write that letter to the Roziers. The same way they forced her to call her mother and say everything was fine."

10

A Telltale Clue

"You mean, all that stuff about Phoenix and going to museums isn't true?" Bess asked, looking puzzled.

"It's very possible," Nancy replied. "I think Kim put that stuff in the letter, hoping someone who knew her well would see it and know that something major was wrong. Her letter was a cry for help."

"Do you still think Hank has something to do with Kim's disappearance?" George asked worriedly.

Nancy nodded. "More than ever," she said. "The plaid shirt was proof, and I have a hunch that Henry Sinclair is Hank Meader's real name."

"But why would Henry Sinclair change his name to Hank Meader?" Bess asked.

"Because," Nancy explained, "if Laurent

94

and Pierre Dennon are actually the same man, Pierre never would have hired a man whose name he recognized from the legal suit that destroyed his company."

"I still don't get it," Bess said, shaking her head. "If Henry thought Pierre's cosmetics had blinded his daughter, why would he want to work for Pierre?"

"When you work for someone," Nancy said slowly, "you're with him or her every day. You learn their habits, their strengths and weaknesses . . ."

"I see what you mean," George said with a shudder. "It's the perfect setup."

"For what?" Bess wailed.

Nancy smiled sadly. "For planning and executing the perfect revenge."

Bess sat down hard on the bed, her blue eyes wide. "That's awful," she said.

"I have a feeling Hank's been sabotaging the spa for a while now," Nancy went on. "He may even be blackmailing the Roziers. That's probably the real reason for all the heavy-duty security patrols. The Roziers probably have no idea who's out to get them."

"But if Hank's after the Roziers, why would he kidnap Kim?" George asked.

"Maybe because she discovered that he was behind the sabotage," Nancy said. "And he couldn't risk letting her ruin things for him."

"So where is Kim now?" Bess asked. "She could be in terrible danger."

"I don't think Hank's got her on the grounds of the spa," Nancy said slowly. "I have an awful feeling she's a long way from Solaire."

"Maybe it's time to go to the police," George said.

Nancy nodded. "But first, I'd like to have a talk with Jacqueline."

Jacqueline didn't return to Solaire until nearly three that afternoon. When she entered the office, Nancy was waiting for her. "Could I speak with you alone for a few minutes?" Nancy asked. "It's very important."

With a shrug, Jacqueline showed Nancy into her private office. The entire room was decorated in ivory and pale desert greens.

On Jacqueline's desk was a vase filled with fragrant white lilies. Like Jacqueline herself, the room was cool and elegant and perfectly beautiful.

"Would you like some mineral water?" Jacqueline asked, opening a wooden cabinet that concealed a small refrigerator.

"Thanks," Nancy said, accepting a glass.

"Now, what is so urgent?" Jacqueline asked. "You know that it is very important to us that all of our guests are happy at Solaire."

Nancy took a deep breath. "I know the spa is being sabotaged," she began. "And I know

96

who's responsible. I think you have to go to the police right away, before someone else gets hurt."

Jacqueline gave Nancy a thin smile. "Surely things cannot be as dire as all that."

"My friend was knocked unconscious, another guest pulled a ligament, Rhonda Wilkins and I were almost killed, and Kim's been kidnapped!" Nancy said urgently. "What more are you waiting for?"

"Kim is fine," Jacqueline said calmly. "I showed you her letter yesterday and—"

"And if you knew anything about her, you'd realize that that letter was a call for help," Nancy broke in. "Kim hates Phoenix, and she never goes to museums. Someone forced her to write that letter. She put those things in as a kind of distress signal."

"Ms. Drew," Jacqueline said calmly, "I am sure you mean well, but this is really none of your business. I believe you have—what do you call it in English?—an overactive imagination."

"And you have a serious problem on your hands," Nancy retorted. "You're going to lose clients if this keeps up. Whitney is threatening lawsuits. Melina was very upset this morning. Even if you don't believe what I'm telling you about Kim, don't you care about Solaire's reputation?"

Jacqueline stood up, her green eyes flashing.

"I have nothing more to say to you, Ms. Drew. Except that, if you wish to continue your stay at Solaire, I strongly suggest you stop all of this meddling."

Nancy stood up, set her glass down, and left Jacqueline's office without another word.

She found George and Bess in one of the outdoor Jacuzzis.

"Come join us for a second," Bess called out. "This water is so relaxing."

"How did your talk with Jacqueline go?" George asked. "What did she say about Kim?"

"The woman didn't pay attention to a word I said," Nancy replied.

"That's terrible," Bess said.

Nancy sighed. "I know. So, how was your afternoon?"

"I went riding," Bess reported, "and Hank was very nice. He's great with the horses. He told me he used to own a ranch."

Just like Henry Sinclair, Nancy thought.

"Then I went back to the gym and had a fitness session with Alain," Bess went on. "Guess what? I've lost another three-quarters of a pound!"

"And I had a tennis game with Lisette," George said. "She's an incredible player."

Nancy felt a sudden twinge of regret. "Now that you guys are having a good time here, I hope I haven't blown it for all of us."

"What do you mean?" Bess asked.

"I took a chance confiding in Jacqueline," Nancy said. "She and Laurent are definitely trying to hide something, and now she knows I'm onto them. So I'm probably not her favorite guest at the moment. I just hope that doesn't make things difficult for you two."

"We'll be okay," George assured her. "If we can survive Alain and the rabbit food they feed us here, we can survive anything."

Nancy appreciated George's effort to make her feel better, but she was still a little worried about her friends. She didn't trust anyone at Solaire, particularly the Roziers, Hank, and Alain. But maybe she was carrying things too far.

"Bess," Nancy said, "do you still think the Roziers and their staff are not involved in any of the things that have been going on?"

Bess eased herself out of the Jacuzzi and hesitated before answering. "I guess the muddy plaid shirt was pretty solid evidence that Hank was down at the falls on the day Kim disappeared," she said finally. "And as for the Roziers and Alain . . . well, they've all been acting kind of strange at times, but the law does say that someone is innocent until proven guilty."

"You're right, Bess," Nancy agreed. "I've got plenty of theories about what's going on here. What I need now is solid proof."

99

"Maybe we'd better change the subject," George said quietly.

Alain was walking toward them. "What's going on here?" he called out in a teasing voice. "I turn my back for a few minutes, and all three of you get lazy?"

"It's a matter of balance," George told him. "You know—work, play. Exercise, relax. Vegetables, chocolate."

"I see," Alain said, his tone amused. "Well, I'm on my way to the pool. I'll be teaching a water aerobics class in thirty minutes. I expect to see you all there."

George got out of the Jacuzzi and reached for a towel. "That man can even make swimming sound like work. At least tonight will be all play."

"That's right," Nancy said. "I forgot we were taking a trip to Old Tucson tonight. I never really thought I'd be that interested in a re-created Wild West town, but nowadays the idea of going anywhere they serve normal food . . ."

"Hot dogs and hamburgers and french fries," George said dreamily.

"Butterscotch sundaes and devil's food cake," Nancy added. "And honey-dipped fried chicken."

Bess stood up, looking extremely self-righteous. "I refuse to be tempted," she said in a lofty tone.

100

Nancy and George grinned at each other. "We'll tell you all about it," George promised.

After the two cousins had gone off to Alain's water aerobics class, Nancy decided to take a walk around the grounds. She didn't have much hope of finding any clues, but she needed to sort through the facts she had.

Nancy headed north, walking toward the Catalina Mountains. She enjoyed seeing the play of light and shadow on the slopes. The mountains seemed to change with the course of the sun, as if every time she looked at them, they showed her different parts of themselves. Nancy stopped, amused, as a roadrunner darted across her path, its little legs stretching full-length with each stride.

She was just nearing the stables when Hank Meader rode up to her on a bay gelding. "Afternoon, Ms. Drew," he said, reining in the horse.

"Hi," Nancy said, surprised he'd stopped.

"You know," Hank drawled, "all sorts of strange things happen out west. Things disappear from one place, reappear in another. Some folks say it's pack rats. Others blame the wind."

"What are you talking about?" Nancy asked, suddenly wary.

"For example," he went on, as if he hadn't heard her question, "just this morning I happened to look down and find this."

Nancy's heart raced as he reached into his pocket and took out the delicate silver bracelet Ned had given her.

"'To Nancy with love,'" Hank read. "This wouldn't happen to be yours, now, would it?"

"It was a present from my boyfriend," Nancy said, trying to keep her voice calm. "Thank you for returning it." She reached up to take the bracelet, but Hank pulled it back, just out of her reach.

"I found it on the floor of my bedroom," he said in a soft voice. "Now, like I told you, strange things happen out west, so I'm not going to make a big deal of this."

Nancy felt herself starting to shake. She was amazed when Hank simply handed her the bracelet.

"Just a warning, Ms. Drew. Don't let any more of your things 'disappear' into my house. Not only won't you get it back, but I promise you, missing jewelry will be the least of your problems."

11

A Dangerous Mission

All during the ride to Old Tucson, Nancy's mind was on the case. She barely noticed when the van began the nearly vertical descent through Gates Pass to the other side of the Tucson Mountains.

Nancy's concentration was focused on Hank Meader, who was driving the van. Instinct told her that Hank Meader was really Henry Sinclair, but how was she ever going to prove it? Should she break into his house again and search until she found some piece of identification for Henry Sinclair? That probably wasn't the best idea, she decided. Not after he'd found her bracelet in his room.

Maybe she ought to forget all about double identities and simply concentrate on finding Kim Foster. She could go to the police with the photograph showing the spot of plaid, but how

103

would they weigh that against a cheerful letter signed in Kim's own handwriting? Where was Kim now? Nancy wondered. Was she safe? Scared? Was it possible she'd escaped on her own?

Hank pulled the van into the Old Tucson parking lot. So many of the spa guests had wanted to go on this field trip that Solaire had sent another van driven by Lisette, and a station wagon driven by Alain.

"Talk about atmosphere," George said to Nancy as they got out of the van. She nodded toward the uneven ocotillo fence that bordered the area. "They even made the parking lot look like an Old West stockade."

The Solaire group passed through the entry gate and stood back as a brightly painted steam locomotive chugged by. Crossing over the tracks, they entered a dusty street lined with two-story wooden buildings and hitching posts. Actors dressed as gunfighters, cavalry soldiers, and dancers walked the streets, mingling with the tourists.

"This place looks awfully familiar," Bess said in a puzzled tone.

"That's probably because you've seen it in dozens of movies and TV shows," Hank explained. "Besides being an amusement park, Old Tucson is a soundstage. Hollywood's been shooting westerns here since 1939."

Nancy nodded toward a roped-off side street

with a sign reading Hot Set. "Does that mean they're actually shooting now?"

"That's right, ma'am," drawled a handsome young man dressed as a gunfighter. He tipped his hat to Nancy. "In approximately fifteen minutes you can watch me hold up the stagecoach. It's a great scene. I set the stagecoach on fire, and then it rolls down a cliff."

Alain made his way to the front of the group. "You're all free to explore on your own, as long as you're back in the parking lot by nine P.M."

"I'm heading straight for the Coyote Cafe," George vowed. "Junk food, here I come!"

Alain raised one disapproving eyebrow but didn't comment.

"I'm with you, George," Mr. Harper said, sounding extremely relieved to have found a kindred soul.

His wife took his arm. "So am I. I've been good about as long as I can stand it."

"Not me," Bess said, sounding wistful. "I think I'll just walk around and check out the sights."

Nancy was very tempted by the idea of a junk-food binge. But she was more determined to learn anything she could about Hank Meader. Then again, she thought as she watched George and most of the other Solaire guests set off for the cafe, how much can I learn about anyone by following him around an amusement park?

105

Nancy dropped back a short distance and let Hank walk ahead of her. Melina Michaels was at his side, and the two of them seemed to be talking quietly. Bess, unsurprisingly, set off with Alain. Nancy wished she could trail both Alain and Hank at once.

Melina and Hank make an odd pair, Nancy thought. Melina wore a flowing skirt and a wide-brimmed hat, and Hank had on his usual work clothes. She's so elegant and sophisticated; he looks like a cowboy living in Old Tucson. Melina Michaels had revealed very little about herself to anyone. What could she and Hank possibly have in common? Don't be a snob, Nancy told herself.

Nancy followed the pair through the dusty streets. They wound in and out of the old doctor's office, the saloon, the bank, the schoolhouse, and the store selling western wear. Melina and Hank stopped to read the signs explaining which movies had been filmed where. They bought sodas. They acted like all the other tourists. Nancy was beginning to think that trailing Hank was a colossal waste of time. Still, she wasn't ready to give up.

A voice over the PA system announced that a gunfight was about to take place in front of Doc's Apothecary. Nancy watched as Melina and most of the other guests from Solaire congregated in front of the apothecary. Hank,

106

however, said something to Melina and slipped away, moving in the opposite direction.

Finally! Nancy thought. She followed Hank through the crowds until they reached the side street that had been roped off for filming. To Nancy's surprise, Hank paid no attention to the signs. He walked straight into the roped-off area as if he were part of the movie crew.

The set itself was empty. Like the main street of town, the side street was edged with a line of narrow wooden buildings connected by a rickety-looking second-floor balcony. Across from the buildings was a long watering trough. And at the very end of the street was a fountain and an old Spanish-style mission. An empty stagecoach stood at the side of the mission.

Nancy watched, fascinated, as Hank walked up to the mission, opened the heavy wooden front doors, and let himself in. Was he meeting someone? Was this where Kim Foster was being held?

Nancy glanced around at the empty plaza, then up at the church bell tower. She'd love to ring it and alert someone. Then again, she could always go for help—there were crowds of people nearby on the main street. But if she did that, she might lose Hank.

Quietly, Nancy approached the front of the building. One of the heavy wooden doors was still ajar. She peered inside the church and saw

107

only darkness. She'd have to go in if she wanted to know what Hank Meader was up to.

Moving as carefully as she could, Nancy inched the door open and stepped inside. She looked around the dark, high-ceilinged room. It was difficult to believe that the old mission wasn't a real church. Candles set in the walls revealed hardwood pews, an altar, and statues of saints. The chapel was hushed and empty. Hank Meader was nowhere to be seen.

Nancy spotted a small door on the back wall. Walking silently, she made her way toward it. Suddenly, a powerful hand clamped down hard over Nancy's mouth, and another hand pinned her arms behind her.

Nancy fought with all her strength, but in a matter of seconds, a gag was slipped into her mouth and her wrists were bound behind her. She continued to struggle, determined to at least see her captor's face, but her hopes faded as a blindfold was tied quickly over her eyes.

Then Nancy was slung up over someone's shoulder, and the person began to carry her somewhere. Light passed through the blindfold, and Nancy knew they'd left the dark interior of the mission. Finally, Nancy heard some sort of door open, and she was tossed onto a hard wooden surface. The door shut again, and footsteps hurried away.

For a long time, everything was silent, except for the sounds of the faraway shootout and the clapping crowd. Nancy strained uselessly against the ropes.

The next thing she heard was the sound of the horses whinnying. Where am I? Nancy wondered. A barn? A stable?

Then the floor beneath her rocked suddenly, and Nancy felt herself roll against something hard. The horses nickered, and a man gave a gruff call. Then the floor beneath her began to move again.

The stagecoach! Nancy realized. I must be on the floor of the coach. Where was it going to take her? She remembered the actor she'd met earlier saying he was going to hold up a stage, and she prayed it would be the same one. Maybe she could get help.

But the stagecoach rolled on and on, and Nancy didn't hear any more voices. It didn't seem as if they were driving into the middle of a movie set, and they hadn't turned onto the main street of the town. Nancy's heart sank. She was probably being taken somewhere off the grounds of Old Tucson and into the surrounding mountains.

Her hopes grew even fainter as the stage came to a quick halt and she heard Hank Meader's voice. "Make sure the stunt works," he ordered someone. "When you hear the gunshot, that will be the signal. Release the pin and steer the horses to the right. You'll have plenty of room to turn and get them stopped."

109

"What about the stage?" the other man asked.

"The stagecoach will be set on fire," Hank replied. "It's in the script. And then it will roll down the cliff. Old Tucson is going to have one less stagecoach in its stable."

Nancy couldn't believe what she was hearing. The stagecoach would be set on fire with her in it!

"Goodbye, Ms. Drew," Hank Meader said, sounding closer. "Think of it this way. You'll be the first guest at Spa Solaire to die in a stagecoach disaster."

12

Changing Gears

"Stagecoach scene, take one!" a woman's voice called.

Lying in the bottom of the stagecoach, gagged, blindfolded, and bound, Nancy desperately did her best to make noise and call attention to herself. She had to stop this scene before the coach was set on fire!

Suddenly, Nancy heard the sound of a whip being cracked in the air. The driver of the coach called out a command to the team of horses. Nancy jounced hard across the floor as the coach began to roll.

There has to be a way out of this, she thought frantically. She knew there was a door to the coach. She just had to find a way to open it, but she was totally unable to move.

Nancy told herself that she had to try. Scooting her body across the floor, she managed to get to her knees. The coach rattled on. It was hard to keep her balance, but Nancy used her elbows to search for the side of the coach. After what seemed like endless minutes of probing in the dark, she felt a thin line of cool air on her face. She'd found the door! Now all she had to do was find a way to open it.

Nancy angled her body so that her feet pressed against the door. Then she kicked at it as hard as she could. The door didn't move.

Nancy heard the driver crack the whip again, and the horses' hooves pounded against the dirt, breaking into a headlong gallop. Soon the driver would release the pin, and the horses would be driven off. The coach would roll free and someone would set it on fire. Using every ounce of strength she had, Nancy kicked at the door again. This time she felt a rush of air. The door was open!

Nancy's heart raced. Did she have the courage for what she had to do next? She had no choice. She had to throw herself from the moving stagecoach.

Nancy struggled toward the door, then froze. How could she throw herself from a racing stagecoach?

Then the signal shot cracked through the air, louder even than the sound of the horses' hooves.

Without a second thought, Nancy hurled

herself through the open coach door. She landed in soft dirt, rolling over and over.

She heard someone rush to her side, and then a baffled man's voice, asking, "What—?"

"Never mind what," said a crisp woman's voice. "Let's get these ropes off her."

Seconds later, the blindfold fell away. The gag and ropes soon followed. Nancy sat up and slowly began to rub the feeling back into her wrists and ankles. She was sore and covered with dirt, but relieved to be alive.

"Who are you?" asked the man who'd cut the ropes. "And what were you doing in my movie?"

"I was in a movie?" Nancy asked. Somehow, that fact hadn't quite sunk in.

"Not for long," the woman said, smiling. "I'm afraid there's no rational explanation in our story for having a teenage girl tied up in the back of the coach. Sorry, but we probably won't be using your footage." She held out her hand to Nancy. "I'm Bonnie Walker, the producer. Are you all right?"

"Fine, I think," Nancy said shakily, getting to her feet.

"What happened to you?" demanded a familiar voice. It was Alain, with Bess and George right behind him. "We've been looking all over for you," the trainer added.

"The one we ought to be looking for is Hank

113

Meader," Nancy informed him, brushing herself off. "He put me in that stagecoach."

Bess's faced paled. "I just saw Hank heading for the parking lot."

"We've got to catch him," Nancy said quickly. "Bess, can you go get security and call the police? George, let's go!"

Nancy and George set off at a run, ignoring Alain's demands for an explanation.

Every bone in Nancy's body ached by the time she and George reached the parking lot. The fall from the stagecoach had left her entire body bruised. But she forced herself on, determined to stop Hank.

Ahead of her, she spotted Hank in the driver's seat of one of the Solaire vans. Nancy's heart sank as she heard the engine turn over.

"He's getting away!" Alain said.

In her mad rush to the parking lot, Nancy hadn't even noticed that the trainer was following them, but since he was, maybe she could get him to help. "Alain, please," she said. "I need the keys to the station wagon."

"I can't give you the keys," he replied at once.

Nancy watched helplessly as the van started up and Hank pulled out of the parking space. Fortunately, there was a line of other cars ahead of him, also on their way out.

She turned to Alain again. "You don't understand," she said pleadingly. "Hank is a black-mailer, a kidnapper, and he nearly committed murder today. We've got to catch him!"

Alain pulled the car keys from his pocket and grabbed Nancy by the arm. "Well, then, let's go," he said, starting toward the station wagon.

This wasn't what Nancy had planned. Alain could be in cahoots with Hank. There was no way she was going to get into a car with him.

She signaled to George, who had overheard the conversation. Quickly, George dropped to the ground. "Oww!" she cried. "I think I sprained my ankle!"

Alain paused and looked down at George in concern. But before the trainer could even ask what was wrong, George's foot shot out, sweeping Alain's feet from under him.

The keys flew from Alain's hand. Nancy scooped them up instantly and ran to the car with George right behind her. The two of them got in and locked the doors. "I'm afraid to look," Nancy said to George, starting the engine. "Is Hank still in the parking lot?"

"He's about two cars away from the entrance," George reported. "But there's no one behind him. We ought to be able to catch him."

Nancy backed up as fast as she dared, then sped out of the parking lot.

Something large flew into Nancy's line of vision, and suddenly Nancy was face-to-face with Alain, who had jumped onto the hood of the car.

Nancy was so alarmed to see Alain scowling angrily at her that she slammed on the brakes, hard. Alain's furious expression turned to one of panic as the sudden force of the brakes threw him from the hood of the car.

13

The Middle of Nowhere

Nancy threw the car into park and looked over at George. "Do you think he's hurt?" she said, her eyes wide with fear.

Quickly, the two girls jumped out of the car and ran around to the front. Alain was lying motionless on the ground.

Worriedly, Nancy bent over the fallen trainer. All of a sudden, Alain jumped up and grabbed Nancy by the shoulders.

"You're a crazy, stupid kid," he cried, shaking her. "What do you think you're doing, getting in my way?"

"*Your* way!" Nancy said indignantly as she pulled away from Alain.

George took a step toward Alain and said, "Don't put a hand on her!"

Nancy watched, helpless, as Hank's van shot forward, then turned right.

117

"Then keep out of my way," Alain retorted. "The Roziers hired *me* as their bodyguard. Someone was blackmailing them for the last year, and then the blackmailer started demanding more money—or else. When the Roziers didn't comply, the sabotage at the spa started. Jacqueline feared for their lives. She figured that the blackmailer had to be either on the spa grounds or working with someone on the inside. That's when Laurent contacted me, and they put on all that extra security."

Nancy was surprised to hear that Alain had been hired as a bodyguard, but it did explain why his actions had seemed so suspicious to her. She wasn't completely sure that the trainer was telling the truth, and a glance over at George told Nancy that her friend felt the same way.

"I caught on to Hank Meader's tricks right away," Alain continued. "I've been following him for weeks, trying to catch him in the act. But then *you* had to foul everything up, Nancy Drew."

"I knew you weren't a real trainer," George said.

"No, but my father was one," Alain said, "for a college football team. I grew up in France with an exercise regimen that makes Solaire's routine look like an afternoon nap. And I'm a pretty good amateur detective, too."

118

"Spare us," George murmured.

"I tried," Alain went on. "But you kept getting in the way, Nancy Drew. I never expected you to try anything as crazy as breaking into Hank Meader's house. What did you think you were doing?"

"Trying to find Kim Foster," Nancy replied evenly. "Did you even realize she's been kidnapped?"

"Why don't we all stop arguing and try to help each other?" George said. "Hank Meader just pulled out of the parking lot."

Without another word, Alain, Nancy, and George all piled back into the Solaire station wagon. "Go to the left," Alain told Nancy, "and then north on Silverbell."

"Why?" Nancy asked. She knew George was right. She and Alain ought to be sharing information and helping each other, but she still found it hard to trust him.

"Because," Alain said, with an obvious attempt at patience, "that's where Hank Meader has another house."

"Are you sure?" Nancy asked.

"Positive."

Nancy followed Alain's precise directions to a narrow dirt road on the north side of the Tucson Mountains, about fifteen miles outside the city.

"This is more like a footpath than a road,"

119

George observed as Nancy slowed the car to negotiate the overgrown trail. Carefully, she steered around a large rock, then gasped as the front wheel sank into a small ditch.

"Keep going," Alain said. "The car will pull through."

Nancy rode the car out of the ditch. Darkness was falling fast. She peered out through the windshield.

"Does anyone really live up here?" she asked. "I don't see a single house. Who could deal with this road every day?"

"The road isn't a problem for a pickup truck," Alain pointed out, "which is what Hank normally drives. Keep going. He's farther into the mountains."

"Have you actually been to this place?" George asked, frowning.

"I drove up here one day last week," Alain said. "I just walked around the outside of the place." He gave Nancy a wry glance. "Unlike some people, I'm not fond of breaking and entering."

"It was necessary," Nancy said evenly. "Anyway, I didn't break in—the window was open. And I found proof that Hank was at the falls the day Kim Foster disappeared. I think he kidnapped her because she knew he was sabotaging the spa."

"You may be right," Alain said quietly. "I had suspicions about that myself, because

Hank mysteriously had to go into town that day. I just hope we're not too late now."

Nancy winced as the car dipped down into another deep rut and rumbled out. The road bent sharply to the right and seemed to narrow even more.

"There!" Alain said suddenly.

Nancy hit the brakes. "Where?" she asked, peering out into the darkness. "I don't see a thing, except lots of cacti."

"Turn the lights off," Alain said. "Unless you *want* Hank to see you. Actually, maybe we'd better walk the rest of the way. If he's there, he'd hear the car. Pull off the road."

"What road?" Nancy muttered, but she did as Alain had asked. "Are you sure there's a house up here?" she asked.

"It's about a quarter of a mile past where the road bends to the right," Alain said, getting out of the station wagon.

Nancy and George followed Alain as he made his way through high grasses and prickly pear cacti. I sure hope we can trust this guy, Nancy thought with a shiver. Because if Alain wasn't telling the truth, she and George were alone with him in one of the most deserted spots she'd ever seen.

After they'd walked another ten minutes, Alain pointed to a small, dark house at the crest of a hill.

"I don't see the van," Nancy said doubtfully.

"Hank may not be here," Alain replied. "That doesn't mean it's not worth checking the cabin for Kim."

"Let's go," George said immediately.

Alain put a finger to his lips and shut off his flashlight. "We're going to have to work by moonlight from now on."

The three carefully approached the house. Then Alain signaled the girls to wait while he circled around it.

"I don't think anyone's in there," he reported when he came back. "At least, not anyone who's awake."

"I'll try the front door, if you'll try the back," Nancy offered.

Alain nodded, and Nancy and George walked up to the front entrance, wondering if anyone was inside. The place seemed completely deserted. Nancy knocked on the door. No answer. She pushed at the door and nearly fell forward when it opened.

"I guess if you live this far out in the boonies, you don't worry about locking up," George said.

To Nancy, that was a bad sign. Surely, if Kim were being hidden there, the door would be locked.

Using their flashlights, Nancy and George began to walk through the small house. The inside was furnished with a kitchen table and two chairs, a ratty couch, and a TV. A tiny bedroom held a narrow twin bed. In the bathroom, Nancy saw a tube of toothpaste, a toothbrush, and a single bottle of shampoo. She looked around for mail or something that might have the owner's name and address. There was nothing. And there was definitely no sign of Kim.

"Nancy," George whispered, "where do you think this door leads?"

"Good question," Nancy said. She shone her flashlight along the length of the door. About two feet above the doorknob was a latch secured with a padlock. Nancy frowned. "I wonder why there's a lock on it."

Nancy examined the padlock, then reached into the pocket of her jeans for the narrow pick she usually carried. It didn't work on all locks, but it was worth trying on this one.

Nancy held her breath as she inserted the pick in the base of the padlock and wiggled it. She felt a familiar sense of excitement as the lock suddenly popped open. Carefully, she lifted it from the latch and led the way downstairs.

The basement was even darker than the upstairs had been. The hairs on the back of Nancy's neck rose as she heard the steady, unmistakable sound of breathing. She turned to George behind her, but the sound wasn't coming from her friend. And since they'd entered the house, neither of them had seen Alain.

They were in the pitch-black basement of a house that was miles from nowhere. *And someone else was in there with them!*

14

In the Dark

"Nan?" George's voice was a tense whisper. "Do you hear that?"

Nancy nodded, not trusting herself to move. If she turned on her flashlight, which was what she was tempted to do, she'd know who else was in the dark basement. She might also be turning herself and George into illuminated targets.

The breathing continued, steady, rhythmical, and deep. It occurred to Nancy that whoever was in the basement with them was asleep.

She was about to turn on her flashlight when she heard someone walking above them.

"That better be Alain," George said in a low voice.

"It is," Alain said as he opened the door to

the basement and joined them on the stairs. "Why are you two standing here?"

"Shhh," Nancy said, turning on her flashlight and slowly descending the stairs. The beam of her light roamed over piles of cardboard boxes, a hard-backed chair, a small table with an empty plate and mug on it, and a narrow cot. Kim Foster was sleeping on the cot, her wrists and ankles tied with bandannas.

"Kim!" Nancy was beside her at once, shaking her gently. "Kim, wake up. We've come to get you out of here."

Kim opened her eyes drowsily. "Who—? What?" she said.

"It's Nancy Drew, from Solaire, with George and Alain," Nancy said quickly. "Let me see your wrists. George, could you hold the light while I unknot this thing?"

Kim sat silently as Nancy worked on her bonds. Kim was definitely paler and thinner than she'd been when they'd seen her last. Within seconds, Nancy had freed her wrists and ankles.

"Are you all right?" Alain asked, sitting beside her.

"I think so," Kim said in a shaky voice. "I haven't been hurt, just kept tied up in the dark. He's only let me walk to the bathroom. I feel a little weak."

"He?" Nancy asked. "You mean Hank Meader?"

Kim rubbed at her ankles and rose to her feet unsteadily. "It was Hank, all right," she said, her voice bitter. "I'll explain everything, I promise. But right now, could we please get out of here? I can't spend another minute in this awful basement."

"Of course," Alain said. "Let me help you."

But they were too late. As the four of them started toward the stairs, the door to the basement slammed shut. Nancy felt a band of fear tighten around her chest. Someone was locking the padlock!

George raced to the top of the stairs. "Let us out!" she screamed, pounding against the door. "Let us out *now!*"

Alain went to George's side. "That won't do any good," he told her gently. "Don't waste your energy."

Beside Nancy, Kim collapsed to the floor. She drew her knees up to her chest and hid her head in her arms. She was crying softly.

"Kim." Nancy knelt beside her, trying to comfort her.

"We're never going to get out of here," Kim sobbed. "We had our chance and we lost it. Now I'll never be free. I'm never going to see the sun or the sky—"

"Of course you will," Nancy said with more confidence than she felt. "We're all going to come through this just fine. There are four of us

127

and only one Hank Meader. We'll figure something out."

"Like what?" George asked.

"I don't know," Nancy admitted. "Let's just try to calm down for a bit."

"The first thing we should do is see if there's any other way out of this basement," Alain said. "If you'll let me borrow your flashlight, Nancy, I'll see what I can find."

Nancy handed him the light, and Alain began to explore the cellar.

"So," Nancy said, wanting to keep Kim distracted, "what exactly did happen that day at the falls?"

"Hank followed us down there," Kim replied. "He'd been sabotaging the spa. The day before you arrived, I'd caught him deliberately tampering with the heat controls on the Jacuzzi. That's what I wanted to talk to you about."

"Why didn't you tell the Roziers?" George asked.

Kim sighed. "Because before then, I'd always liked Hank. We were friends. I didn't want him to be fired. But there'd been other strange things going on at the spa, and when I caught Hank at the Jacuzzi I realized he'd probably been responsible for all of them. I told him I wouldn't say anything to the Roziers if he'd just stop what he was doing."

"And he didn't believe you?" George asked grimly.

Kim shrugged and rubbed her eyes. "I guess he couldn't afford to take the chance that I'd change my mind. Since the Roziers had already tightened security measures, he was afraid to go after me while we were on the spa grounds. So he followed us to Tanque Verde Falls. He grabbed me when I crossed the creek, right before the flood hit."

Kim gave a little shiver and went on. "In a weird way, Hank saved my life. If he hadn't kidnapped me then, I probably would have been swept downstream by the floodwaters."

"Do you know why Hank was sabotaging Solaire in the first place?" Nancy asked.

"I think I have a good idea," Kim replied. "When Hank first locked me down here, I wasn't tied up, so I poked around a bit." She nodded to the boxes stacked against the wall. "In the bottom one, there's an old newspaper clipping about a court case. There's also a bunch of legal papers between Henry and Heather Sinclair and Jeunesse, a French cosmetics company. Half of them are in French, so I didn't get the whole story, but—"

"Henry Sinclair is Hank Meader's real name," Alain spoke up from the other side of the basement. "And Jeunesse was Laurent Rozier's first cosmetics company. Hank has been trying to pay him back for his daughter Heather's blindness ever since."

"I thought you were working *for* the Roziers," Nancy said, surprised.

"I am," Alain replied. "But while I was snooping around at the spa, I uncovered very unpleasant things in Laurent's past. There are still people suffering because Laurent Rozier cut costs by lying about the safety tests he claimed his cosmetics had undergone."

"Do you have proof of Laurent's connection to Jeunesse?" George asked.

"Unfortunately, no." Alain emerged from the other side of the basement, brushing off his hands. "Bad news," he said. "There are no windows, and no other doors. Just dirt walls. The only way out of this basement is up those stairs."

"Can we break down the door?" Kim asked anxiously.

"With what?" Alain asked.

"Maybe if we all pushed against it . . ." George suggested. "Sort of like a human battering ram."

"Unless someone has a better idea, I think it's worth a try," Nancy said. "It beats just sitting here, feeling helpless."

"Count me in," Kim said.

The four of them lined up on the stairway behind Alain. "All right," he said. "On the count of three, push. One, two, three . . ."

Everyone pushed as hard as he or she could, but the door didn't budge.

"Hank!" Alain called out. "Kidnapping Kim was bad enough. Holding four of us captive is the sort of stunt that will land you a long term in prison. Come on, open the door, before you make things worse for yourself."

But it wasn't Hank who answered. On the other side of the door, a woman's high-pitched voice dissolved into hysterical laughter. "So how do *you* like being in darkness?" she asked. "Do you enjoy being unable to see?"

Chills raced through Nancy as she realized who was speaking. "It's Heather," she told the others in a low voice. "Heather Sinclair."

"Very good," crooned the voice on the other side of the door. "You win a prize for correctly identifying me. Do you want to know what that prize is?"

"I'm not sure we do," George muttered.

"Heather, listen to me," Nancy urged. "We know Laurent Rozier is responsible for your blindness. We're going to see that he's brought to justice. But you've got to let us out for us to do that."

Heather began laughing again. "That's very funny. But I've already heard that one. My father lost his ranch paying lawyers who promised the same thing. Now it's time for someone else to pay. Unfortunately, it's going to be the four of you.

"I'll tell you what I've done," Heather went on. "I've put an old sofa in front of the basement door. If any of you touch the door again, I swear I'll set the whole place on fire."

"Heather, please—" Alain began.

But on the other side of the door, they heard Hank's daughter laugh an evil laugh as she struck the first match.

15

A Chilling Invitation

"She means it," Nancy said quickly. "We'd better go back downstairs."

"All right, Heather," Alain called. "We're going downstairs. You can blow out the match now."

They heard the sound of the match being extinguished. "Don't get any cute ideas," Heather warned. "I'll be sitting right on this couch, listening for your every footstep."

"How comforting," George said, as she started down the stairs.

"Get used to the dark," Heather called after them in a sugary voice. "You'll all be in it for a very long time."

Nancy, George, Kim, and Alain settled themselves in the basement. Nancy and Kim sat on the cot, George sat on the chair, and Alain paced the floor.

"We need a plan," Nancy said.

Alain threw up his hands. "I can't believe I let us get trapped like this. I should have known better!"

"Thinking like that won't do us any good," Kim said.

"She's right," George agreed.

Nancy's eye was caught by something in the shadows. "What's that in the corner?" she asked in a low voice. She walked over and turned on her flashlight. The beam was growing dim. I should have changed these batteries, she thought regretfully. Here they were, locked in a dark basement, and she had a flashlight that barely worked. Still, she managed to make out what looked like a couple of sticks covered with cobwebs.

Nancy brushed away the sticky webs and pulled at the first object. "I can't believe it," she said softly. "A hammer!" She pulled out the second one. "And a crowbar, too. Not exactly the perfect tools, but a start."

George stood up on the chair and began running her fingers along the ceiling. "There's got to be a loose board up here somewhere."

"Maybe we should just wait until Heather falls asleep, and then work on the door," Kim suggested. "The problem is, how will we know when she's asleep?"

"We do have one other hope," Nancy said. "Bess was going to call the police."

"Don't count on them coming to the rescue," Alain said dejectedly. "I only knew about this place because I followed Hank here. The police will never find it. If they go looking for Hank, they'll wind up at his house at Solaire—"

"—where they'll find nothing," George finished grimly.

"Okay, back to Plan A," Nancy said with a sigh. "Let's give Heather some time to fall asleep. Then we'll make our escape."

Time passed slowly in the dark basement. It was impossible to tell what time of night it was. Nancy didn't want to use her already-dying flashlight on something as useless as checking her watch. Exhausted, she leaned against the wall and felt her eyes close. It couldn't hurt to catch a few hours of sleep.

Nancy awoke to the raucous howling of coyotes. At first, she heard the high-pitched yips in the distance, as if the animals were far up in the mountains. Then the calls grew closer. It sounded as if there were hundreds of them.

"They must be partying tonight," Kim said with a smile. "According to some of the Native American traditions, Coyote is a trickster, capable of working magic."

"I wish he'd work some magic on Heather," George grumbled.

The animals' howls grew louder and louder. Nancy listened, fascinated by the strange, wild

135

sound. Sometimes the coyotes all sang together. Other times, one started and the others joined in. Occasionally, the coyotes seemed to be singing a call and response.

"It sounds as if they're surrounding the house," Alain said.

"This may be the perfect time for us to start breaking out of here," Nancy said. "If all we can hear is coyotes, then there's a good chance that that's what Heather's hearing, too. Let's just hope they keep howling."

"I think we've got a better chance of avoiding Heather if we work our way through the ceiling," George said. "If we go through the door, we'll definitely wake her."

"Right," Alain said. After determining the farthest point from the basement door, he stood on the chair and used the end of the crowbar to pull gently at the wooden floorboards. Kim and Nancy carried the table over beside him. Then George got up on the table, and using the hammer's claw, she began to help Alain pry the boards loose.

The two worked slowly, taking care to make as little noise as possible. It'll be morning before they're done, Nancy worried. By the time they were ready to climb out, Heather would be wide awake and eating breakfast. At least the coyotes were still howling.

Finally, Alain and George removed three of

the wooden boards. "Who wants to go first?" Alain whispered.

"I will," Nancy volunteered. Alain boosted her up between two floor beams, and she emerged into the tiny kitchen. At least there were windows, and moonlight was streaming in.

Nancy knelt by the hole in the floor and reached out to help Kim up, then George. Alain boosted himself through a few moments later.

Nancy glanced around the room. There were dishes piled in the old-fashioned sink and a small table in the corner. On top of the table were more dishes, some tools, and a kerosene lamp.

"There's a back door," Nancy whispered, leading the way.

She was just turning the knob when a voice behind them said, "You mustn't be in such a hurry to go. I suggest you all stay right where you are, or this whole place goes up in flames."

Nancy froze in her tracks. It was Heather. Their luck had just run out. With a sinking heart, she heard another match being struck.

"Now, I want all of you to be still," Heather ordered. "Not a single move."

Nancy and the others did as they were told.

Heather stood there, holding the kerosene lamp with one hand. In her other hand was the

burning match. "I'm going to spill the kerosene," she said in a low, menacing voice. "And
then set this place on fire. I don't care if we *all*
die. My life isn't worth living anymore, anyway."

"Heather—" Alain began.

Suddenly, the match went out. Heather
cried out in annoyance and reached for her
pocket.

Seeing her chance, Nancy sprang forward,
followed immediately by Alain, Kim, and
George. Nancy grabbed the deranged girl's
wrist, but Heather swung out at Nancy with
her other arm, knocking the lamp against
Nancy's head. Nancy felt a dull pain in her
head as the sickening smell of kerosene as-
saulted her nostrils. Then the moonlight began
to fade as Nancy crumpled to the floor.

The next thing Nancy knew, the bright glare
of headlights was flashing through the window.
Where am I? she thought. Vaguely, she heard
George calling her name. Then she realized
that her friend was kneeling over her.

"Nancy," George said anxiously. "Are you
okay?"

Nancy nodded, touching her throbbing
head. "I think so," she said. Then she frowned,
remembering. "Where's Heather?"

"She's right here," Alain called from the
corner of the kitchen. "And it's all over. I've
got her pinned."

Then Nancy heard the sound of car doors slamming, and Hank Meader's voice filled the room, funneled through a megaphone.

"Heather," he called, his voice pleading. "I want you to come outside."

"No!" the blind girl shouted, struggling against Alain.

Hank's voice nearly broke. "Heather, the police are here. They've got the house surrounded. You've got to come out now, honey."

Nancy quickly looked out the window. "It's true," she told Heather, relief in her voice. "There are four police cars out there, and the officers are on their way in."

The blind girl's shoulders slumped as the door to the house opened.

"Heather!"

The girl turned at the sound of her father's voice, and Nancy was glad Heather couldn't see that he was handcuffed to the police officer who'd brought him in.

Bess rushed past them. "Nan, George, are you all right?" she cried. "I'm sorry it took us so long. The police were staking out Hank's house at Solaire, but he never showed up. For a while, we didn't think he'd come back to the spa, either. But one of the horses was sick, and it wouldn't let anyone else near it. Hank sneaked back to give it its medication."

"And that's when the police caught him?" Kim asked.

Bess nodded. "He confessed to everything —all the sabotage at the spa, even the black widow spider. Hank trapped Nancy in the mission, too, and put her in the stagecoach. And, of course, he's guilty of kidnapping. He said he forced Kim to write that letter saying she was going to Phoenix. He also made her call her mother, just as you thought, Nancy."

Nancy looked at Hank. He was holding his now-sobbing daughter with his one free arm, trying to comfort her. "Please go easy on her," he said to the police. "Ever since she lost her sight, she hasn't been the same."

Another officer stepped forward and said, "We'll need the rest of you to follow us to the station house for statements."

The first police officer then began to lead Hank and Heather to a squad car. Heather mumbled something inaudible as she walked away. It sounded to Nancy as if the girl had said, "It's not over yet."

"Wait a minute!" Nancy called, looking suspiciously at the Sinclairs.

Hank stopped and turned to look at her.

"Tomorrow is Solaire's kickoff party for the new cosmetics line," she said. "Did you also have a little trick planned for that?"

Hank shook his head, but his daughter's sobbing suddenly turned into hysterical laughter. "Why don't you all go to the party and find out?" she said with an evil grin.

16

A Fitting End

Nancy yawned as she opened the door to the casita. It was nearly four in the morning. She, George, Bess, Kim, and Alain had been at the police station for hours while charges were filed against Hank and his daughter.

"What a night!" George said, flopping down on her bed. "I can't wait to go to sleep."

"I don't know if I *can* sleep," Bess said. "I feel sorry for Hank and Heather. I mean, I know what they were doing was wrong and had to be stopped, but they never would have done any of that if they hadn't been so badly hurt in the first place."

Nancy nodded. "I'm sure the judge will take that into consideration." She looked at Bess curiously. "Does this mean you believe the Roziers are responsible for the whole Jeunesse scandal?"

141

Bess looked uncomfortable. "I'm still not sure Jacqueline was involved, but from what Alain told the police, it seems pretty definite that Laurent was." She sighed. "When I think of all the Solaire products I sold, and how I told everyone how great they were . . ."

"Don't feel bad," Nancy said, putting an arm around her friend's shoulder. "Solaire products may be perfectly safe. The regulations in this country are pretty strict. Besides, Laurent doesn't strike me as the kind of man who makes the same mistake twice. Try to get some sleep," Nancy added. "We'll sort it all out in the morning."

Morning came all too soon. Barely three hours later, at seven A.M., bright spring sunshine streamed into the casita. Outside, the quail and doves were making nearly as much noise as the coyotes had the night before.

Nancy stretched in her bed, planning to go back to sleep. Then she sat bolt upright. She couldn't sleep. She had to tell the Roziers to cancel the promotional party. So far, all the acts of sabotage at the spa had been Hank's. But Nancy had a feeling that whatever was scheduled to happen at the party, if anything, was Heather's plan. And Heather seemed more dangerous than her father.

Nancy got up, took a quick shower, and

142

hurriedly got dressed. She left the casita quietly.

She was halfway to the office when she saw
a sleepy figure stumbling toward the gym.
"Alain!" she called.

He turned, rubbed his eyes, and gave her a
brusque nod. "You'll forgive me if I don't make
polite conversation on three hours of sleep."

"Are you actually going to the *gym* now?"
Nancy asked in disbelief.

He shrugged. "I'm late for a stretch class. I
can't very well leave a gym full of guests to
entertain themselves." He continued on for a
few steps, then stopped in his tracks. "Where
are *you* going?" he asked suspiciously. "Don't
tell me you got up for my stretch class."

"I'm going to talk to the Roziers," Nancy
answered.

Alain caught her by the arm. "Listen to me,"
he said. "Please. I know you want to warn them
about whatever it is that Heather might have
planned for the kickoff party. That's fine. But
please don't accuse Laurent of being Pierre
Dennon."

"Why not?" Nancy asked indignantly. "He *is*
Pierre Dennon. And because of him, Heather
is blind and she and her father are going to
jail."

"If you march into his office with those
accusations, you'll force Laurent to shut you

up," Alain said. "You've already put yourself in enough danger. Let the police handle it. They'll be interrogating the Roziers."

"How are American police going to prosecute a crime that took place in France years ago?" Nancy asked.

Alain shrugged. "There's extradition. And even if that doesn't apply in this case, there are other means for making Pierre Dennon pay." Alain suddenly stopped talking as another spa staff member passed by. "I have to go," he said. "Good luck. And be careful."

"I will," Nancy promised. She crossed the courtyard and entered the office, where she asked to speak to Laurent.

"He's with Jacqueline," the receptionist replied. "Let me tell them you're here."

A few minutes later, Nancy was ushered into Jacqueline's office. Jacqueline sat at her desk, dressed in an immaculately tailored white linen suit. Laurent stood beside her, wearing an elegant black suit over a white T-shirt. Together, they looked like an advertisement for designer clothing.

No, Nancy thought. What they are is an advertisement for wealth and beauty. People are supposed to come to Solaire to look just like them. Everyone is supposed to think the two of them are perfect. But, Nancy reminded her-

144

self, Laurent was responsible for blinding at least one person and doing damage to who knows how many others. And she had a feeling that Jacqueline had helped him cover it up.

"*Bonjour*, Mademoiselle Drew," Laurent said. "How can we help you?"

"Have the police called you?" Nancy asked.

"Indeed," Jacqueline said. "We will be going down to the station later today to press charges against Hank for the sabotage. I am so sorry that you were inconvenienced last night. But, you see, everything has worked out, as I told you it would." She flashed Nancy a dazzling white smile. "There's no longer any reason to worry."

"I don't think the sabotage is over," Nancy said. "Last night, when the police arrested Heather, she hinted at other plans for today's party. You've got to call the whole thing off."

"That's impossible," Laurent said. "The press and some of our most important clients are coming in from New York and L.A. We can't possibly cancel."

"Are you willing to risk someone else's being hurt?" Nancy asked.

"No one else will be hurt," Laurent said firmly. "We will take extra security precautions."

"Your security didn't stop the other accidents," Nancy pointed out.

145

"Ms. Drew," Jacqueline said. "Clearly, this is not your concern. Now, my husband and I have business to discuss. If you will be so kind as to leave us—"

"You don't care," Nancy said quietly. "You don't care about your guests. Or about the truth. The only thing you care about is your perfect image."

Laurent stood up. "Would you like me to escort you out, Mademoiselle Drew?"

"That's all right," Nancy told him. "I can find my own way, thank you very much."

"And I thought *we* were early for the party," George said as she, Bess, and Nancy entered the spa's Ocotillo Hall. The large, airy room was already crowded with people. Guests, staff members, and reporters were all mingling together, many of them drawn to the picture windows that looked out over the mountains. Vases filled with fresh-cut flowers were everywhere, and large wooden tables displayed the new Solaire cosmetics. Other tables were covered with southwestern food specialties.

"*Now* they feed us," Max Harper muttered, as he piled his dish high with hors d'oeuvres. "I'm going to go up to that reporter there and tell him what the normal menu is around here."

"Oh, Max, I'm sure they know this isn't a

146

regular spa meal," said his wife, smiling. "You
did lose four pounds, you know." She leaned
forward and kissed her husband. "It's healthier for you, and you look very handsome."

Nancy smiled as she watched Mr. Harper
blush at his wife's compliment.

Nancy scanned the crowd warily. Rhonda
Wilkins was talking with a group of other
guests, looking more fit and quite pleased with
herself. Lisette, the tennis pro, looked bored
but determined to be polite. Kim wasn't there
at all, which wasn't surprising. She'd told the
girls that she planned to get twelve hours of
sleep and then go visit her mother. There was
no sign of the German shepherds, but Nancy
was sure that some of the Solaire staff was
acting as security. Alain circled the crowd,
watching everyone intently. What had Heather
planned? Nancy wondered. Maybe Heather's
plan would be impossible to pull off, now that
she was in custody. Or had the girl simply been
bluffing?

"I think the official stuff's about to start,"
George said, holding her own heaping plate of
food.

Jacqueline and Laurent Rozier stood at the
microphone at the front of the room. After
Laurent had asked for everyone's attention, he
began to talk about the exciting new line of
Solaire cosmetics. "I developed these in St.

Martin, specifically with the discerning American woman in mind. You will find our products natural, healthy, and affordable."

"An itty-bitty bottle of moisturizer for thirty dollars?" George muttered.

"Sssshhhh," Bess said. "I want to hear this."

Nancy wasn't really listening to the speech. Her eyes were still moving restlessly over the crowd. Hank and his daughter were safely in custody, but Nancy couldn't forget the sound of Heather's evil laugh.

"Now," Laurent went on, "we are proud to give you a preview of our ad campaign, which will appear in all the major magazines." He pointed to an easel beside him, which held what appeared to be several large boards. The top board read Solaire for the Skin, and bore a picture of the spa's sun logo.

With a flourish, Laurent lifted the board to reveal a photograph of a stunning model in an even more stunning swimsuit, applying Solaire sun block.

Then he removed the photograph to show the next one, and a gasp rose from the crowd. This photograph was of a much-younger Laurent Rozier, holding up a bottle of a Jeunesse product. Above the photo, a newspaper headline read, Jeunesse Lawsuit: Charges of Blindness and Disfiguration!

Laurent hurriedly removed the board, only

148

to reveal yet another. This picture showed a very pretty young woman with badly marked skin. A caption read, Pierre Dennon and Jeunesse did this to me.

Laurent's face was purple. "What is this?" he demanded angrily.

Melina Michaels stood up in response. "Which picture don't you recognize, Pierre? The one of yourself, or the one of my sister?"

The crowd started whispering.

"Security!" Laurent called out. "This woman is not feeling well. Please see that she gets back to her room safely."

"I'm fine," Melina said loudly. "The ones who are not fine are the people who believed that Jeunesse cosmetics were safe. You ruined my sister's modeling career. She's the girl on that poster, with the badly damaged skin. She's still living in seclusion in France, afraid to show the world her face. And you blinded Heather Sinclair." She held up a picture of the sightless girl and showed it to the crowd. Everyone gasped.

"Laurent, aren't you going to answer this woman's charges?" one reporter asked.

"We can explain—" Jacqueline began.

"What about those photographs?" another photographer called out. "How do you explain those?"

Suddenly, Nancy understood. The final sur-

149

prise that Heather had promised had nothing to do with endangering guests. This act had one target only: the Roziers. There was no physical danger involved. Melina was simply exposing them in front of the people who mattered to them most. She was simply telling the truth. And whether or not the Roziers were ever prosecuted, their careers in the beauty business were definitely over.

George leaned toward Nancy. "Why didn't Hank and Heather just wait for this press conference?" she said. "Why do you think they were so determined to hurt people?"

"I guess they were just too angry," Nancy replied. "Remember, there'd been at least one newspaper article about the incident, and that didn't change anything for them."

"Well, this explains why Melina didn't trust the Solaire mineral mud," Bess said. She shook her head. "I think I'm going to skip the rest of this party."

That evening, Nancy found Bess outside the casita, staring up at the starlit sky. "Are you all right?" she asked.

"I'm fine," Bess said cheerfully. "I've lost three-and-a-half pounds."

Nancy grinned. "No, I meant about all the things that have gone on here this week."

"I know," Bess said, her tone serious. "I'm glad the Roziers' past caught up with them. But I still think that, in spite of all those awful things Hank did, Solaire is a great spa. I mean, it was good for me to learn how to work out and diet."

"Do you think you'll keep it up when we go back to River Heights?"

Bess laughed. "Following the Solaire program seems to be a full-time occupation. If I kept up this routine, I wouldn't have time for anything else. Besides, I've been thinking about all of this diet business. Maybe weighing a few extra pounds isn't the worst thing in the world."

"It's crazy for people to think they have to look like fashion models," Nancy agreed. "And to be unhappy if they don't."

Bess pointed to a bright star above. "That's Venus, planet of beauty and love." She sighed. "You know, ever since we got here, I've been looking at Jacqueline, thinking I'd give anything to look like her. I guess I figured that if I were that beautiful, everything else in my life would be perfect. And then today I saw her up there in front of everyone, lying about some really horrible things. . . ."

Nancy smiled at her friend. "Oh, Bess, you're a much better person than Jacqueline. I'm glad you're nothing like her."

151

"Nan," Bess said seriously, "there's just one thing I have to ask you. Do you have any of those emergency chocolate bars left?"

"Definitely," Nancy told her with a grin.

The two of them started back to the casita as the song of the coyotes filled the night.